"Ethan—" She sounded breathless, needy. He loved the sound of his name on her li...

"Ethan, we shouldn't do this. This is a really bad idea."

"I know," he muttered, and set his lips to hers.

His taste was dark and cool. Dangerously arousing, impossibly perfect, assaulting her senses. Her hands fisted in his shirt and she made a tiny sound in her throat, a wordless plea for more, and he heard it. Gave it, moving fast as he pressed her against the wall, his hands snaking into her hair as his lips crushed down on hers.

Ethan couldn't get enough of her. He'd never get enough. The thought slammed into him, and gave him the strength to drag his hands from her hair and step away.

He had to—someone had to—because if they didn't end this now...

"We shouldn't do that again," he muttered.

Accidentally educated in the sciences, **KELLY HUNTER** has always had a weakness for fairy tales, fantasy worlds and losing herself in a good book. Husband…yes. Children…two boys. Cooking and cleaning…sigh. Sports…no, not really, in spite of the best efforts of her family. Gardening…yes; roses, of course. Kelly was born in Australia and has traveled extensively. Although she enjoys living and working in different parts of the world, she still calls Australia home.

Visit Kelly online at her website, www.kellyhunter.net.

*Trouble in a Pinstripe Suit** along with *Revealed: A Prince and a Pregnancy* and *Red-Hot Renegade* were finalists for the Romance Writers of America RITA® award, in the Best Contemporary Series Romance category!

*Originally published in the U.K. under the title *Sleeping Partner*

Other titles by Kelly Hunter available in ebook format:

Harlequin Presents Extra®:

TROUBLE IN A PINSTRIPE SUIT

KELLY HUNTER

~ Men Who Won't Be Tamed ~

Harlequin®

TORONTO NEW YORK LONDON
AMSTERDAM PARIS SYDNEY HAMBURG
STOCKHOLM ATHENS TOKYO MILAN MADRID
PRAGUE WARSAW BUDAPEST AUCKLAND

Recycling programs
for this product may
not exist in your area.

ISBN-13: 978-0-373-52859-2

TROUBLE IN A PINSTRIPE SUIT

Previously published in the U.K. as SLEEPING PARTNER

First North American Publication 2012

TROUBLE IN A
PINSTRIPE SUIT

To family

CHAPTER ONE

'MISS FLETCHER?' asked the wizened old doorman, resplendent in a bone-coloured tunic and turban.

Mia nodded, and turned to stare up at the dilapidated hotel before her. The majestic marble columns and crumbling portico plasterwork. The magnificent marble entrance stairs, dulled by age and the passing of many feet...

The tangled mess of overgrown garden...

'Welcome to Penang, Pearl of the Orient,' he said grandly. 'And the Cornwallis Hotel, lustrous heart of colonial Georgetown.'

The hotel was situated in the heart of the island's colonial district, true enough, and had a certain frayed, yesteryear kind of appeal—but *lustrous?* Mia slid the doorman a bemused glance.

'I know what you're thinking,' he said. 'That the hotel is old and much in need of repair. But sixty years ago, when I first started working here, it was indeed a glory to behold.'

'I believe you.'

Rajah, according to his discreetly placed name tag, beamed. 'It could be so again,' he said. 'Love could make it so.'

Love and vast chunks of money.

'Just as soon as the curse is broken.'

'There's a curse?'

'But of course. How else would the hotel come to be in such disrepair?'

'Years and years of neglect?'

'That, too,' he said. 'I'll inform Mr Ethan of your arrival. He's been waiting for you. We all have.' Rajah swept open the door for her. 'Miss Fletcher.'

'Mia,' she said, belatedly wondering how he'd known who she was.

'Miss Mia,' he said, his old eyes shining. 'Welcome home.'

CHAPTER TWO

THIS wasn't home.

No matter what the old doorman had implied, this hotel had never been Mia's home. She'd been raised in Sydney, schooled there; she lived there…in a sleek upmarket apartment overlooking the Harbour Bridge. She'd chosen the apartment for its spectacular harbour views, and because it was located two blocks away from the Fletcher Corp offices, where she spent a great deal of her time. *That* was her home. Not this run-down colonial hotel in a city half a world away.

Even if she *had* just inherited it from the mother she'd never known.

But the old doorman was waiting for her to enter, and his eyes were kind and welcoming. Home or not, this place was hers now, and Mia would do her duty by it.

She was Richard Fletcher's daughter—his only child—and heir to significant corporate wealth. She knew a great deal about duty.

She could do this. She could.

How hard could it be to step into a life she'd never known?

Hard.

But she was used to that, too. With a quick smile for Rajah, Mia took a big breath, squared her shoulders, and stepped inside.

She was the image of her mother. She had the same delicate build, the same hauntingly elfin face as Lily.

Ethan Hamilton stood at the top of the grand stairway and stared down at the woman Rajah ushered into the lobby. He watched from his vantage point, content for the moment to remain unseen, as she stared curiously about the lobby, her gaze lifting skywards—as everyone's did—to the antique chandelier hanging from the ceiling. All six thou-sand hand-cut crystal pieces of it—never mind that it hadn't worked in years. Her lips curved into a smile—more wondrous child than calculating heiress—and Ethan felt his heart stutter.

He watched as Ayah, the ageing duty manager, hurried towards her. Watched Lily's daughter put her hand out in greeting, only to have Ayah clasp it and press it to her wrinkled cheek. She hadn't been expecting that—didn't like it, even though she masked her discomfort well enough. Ayah spoke briefly and Mia Fletcher shook her head, her expression faintly wistful. Whatever the question, the answer was no. She disengaged her hand, tucked a shoulder-length strand of glossy black hair behind her ear, and looked around again.

Would she notice the superb craftsmanship of the intricately carved rosewood balustrades that flanked the grand staircase? Would she see past the threadbare Persian runner to the exquisite colouring of the marble stairs beneath? Could she see the magic? he wondered. Or would she only see tiredness and decay?

She looked at him.

After a long, long moment she started up the stairs. He should have gone down to greet her, should have acted the gentleman rather than the statue, but one glance from her and he'd forgotten how. She gave him a careful neutral smile when she reached him, and held out her hand.

'Mr Hamilton,' she said. 'I'm Mia Fletcher.'

'I know.' He took her small warm hand in his, bracing hard against the jolt of desire that ran through him like a blade. He'd known need before, had taken care to control it. He released her hand abruptly—politeness be damned—but the memory of her touch remained.

'How did you know who I was?' she asked. 'How did Rajah know?'

'You look like your mother.' Except for her eyes. Lily's eyes had been a rich, warm brown. Her daughter's were grey like a winter sky. Cool, wary eyes that weighed and judged with a thoroughness he'd have welcomed had she not been so thoroughly dissecting *him*. Her father's eyes, he thought with a vague recollection of a stern, dark-haired man with eyes of bleakest grey. That was why they looked so familiar.

'You've never seen a picture of her, have you?'

'No.' Those haunting grey eyes darkened. 'I know very little about my mother, Mr Hamilton. Until your solicitors contacted me three days ago I'd have told you she was an orphan, who married my father, gave birth to me, and died shortly after.'

'You thought she was dead all this time?' Ethan stared at her in shock.

'My father now tells me she left us just after I was born. Apparently she'd fallen in love with another man. A widower with a small son.'

He nodded.

'You're the son, aren't you?'

'Yes.' There was nothing else to say.

She squared her shoulders, as if bracing for an attack. 'I wondered...did she...stay...with you and your father?'

'She stayed,' he said quietly, figuring at least some of what was going through her mind. 'She died in his arms six days ago.'

Mia nodded and looked away, as if it hurt to look at him. 'My condolences on your loss.'

His loss. Not hers. 'That's it?'

Her almost imperceptible shrug conveyed confusion rather than nonchalance. 'I don't know you. I never knew my mother. I don't know why she never tried to contact me, and I don't know why she left me this hotel.' She looked towards the chandelier. 'I mean, what am I supposed to *do* with it?'

'That's entirely up to you,' he said, working hard to remain unmoved by her uncertainty. If she wanted to restore it he would help her. Burn it to the ground or sell it outright—he would help with that, too. He'd promised Lily he would. 'I've put together the financials for the last three years for you.' He gestured towards a bulky black folder on a nearby table. 'The hotel loses money; it always has. The hotel and land valuations are at the back.'

'I don't suppose you have any refurbishment estimates handy?' she said after a pause.

'It's all there. You might want to sit down before you start looking at those particular figures. Have a glass of iced water and a fan handy.'

'Oh.' She smiled wryly. 'That much.'

'More. By all means confirm the values and estimates independently, but they're sound. I've arranged for us to meet the solicitor here at noon tomorrow, for a reading of your mother's will. I'm the executor. There aren't any surprises. The hotel is yours, free and clear. There are some small monetary bequests to some of the staff. That's it.'

She took a deep breath, let it out slowly.

'Would you prefer to reschedule?'

'No,' she said faintly. 'Midday's fine.'

He nodded. 'The hotel staff have prepared a suite for you. There's also the northern wing of the top floor. It hasn't been used in years, but if you stay you may wish to make that your residence.' He didn't know how to say what had to be said next with any degree of finesse, so he opted for the direct approach. 'Your parents used to live there.'

'The suite sounds very comfortable,' she said politely. 'Thank you for arranging it.'

Now for an invitation he wasn't at all sure about offering, given that until three days ago she'd known nothing about any of them. But he'd promised that, too. 'My father has also extended an invitation for you to stay with him. He has a home on the other side of the island.'

She stared at him in silence.

'You're also welcome to make use of the Hamilton Group facilities if you ever need them. Our flagship hotel is here in Georgetown—that's where I'm based—but we also have developments in Kuala Lumpur, Singapore, Hong Kong, and mainland China.' She looked confused, he thought. As if she didn't know quite what was being offered. 'My father and I would like you to consider yourself family.'

Too soon. He knew it long before she spoke.

'That's very generous of you,' she said coolly. 'But no.'

'No to what?'

'No to everything. I have a family, Mr Hamilton, such as it is. I also have money, for what it's worth. I'm not looking for more of either.'

'Then why did you come?'

'Because I had to,' she snapped. 'I had a mother I've never known, a father who refuses to talk about her, a dilapidated boutique hotel that's suddenly my responsibility, and a burning need for answers. Tell me, Mr Hamilton, what would you have done?'

Feisty. Lily would have loved her. He smiled a little at that. 'Talk to my father. He can give you answers.'

'No!' She took a deep breath, as if striving for calm. 'Right or wrong, I'm carrying a fair slice of resentment towards your father at the moment. I appreciate his offer of hospitality—it's a pity it didn't come twenty-four years ago—but I don't want it right now. I'll find my own answers.'

'You may not like them,' he warned.

The smile she sent him was decidedly bittersweet. 'I know.'

So her first encounter with Ethan Hamilton could have gone better, thought Mia as she stood in the middle of the hotel room, suitcase at her side. She'd been aiming for composed and businesslike, or at the very least polite. But his lean, beautiful body and dark as night eyes had mesmerised her, his touch had unsettled her, and she'd been hard pressed to remember her name, let alone how to behave.

He'd mentioned her resemblance to her mother and she'd gone on the defensive. Offered hospitality and *family,* she'd headed straight for prickly. Emotional. Although in that regard she figured she had cause to be.

For three days now she'd been trying to come to terms with the notion that her mother hadn't died all those years ago. That her mother had been alive and well these past twenty-four years and not once, not *once,* had she contacted her. If there was loss, that was it. If there was pain, that was why.

She knew *nothing* about her mother. Not a damn thing about the hotel business. And only marginally more about Penang. She felt tired, confused, and way out of her element.

Maybe that was why she couldn't seem to forget Ethan Hamilton's handshake.

Sighing, she ran a hand around the back of her neck, looked around the room, and sighed again. The elaborately plastered fifteen-foot ceiling was cracked and crumbling with age, and rusty plumbing pipes ran the length of two walls alongside some *very* creative electrical wiring. Someone had planned a wall light or five and never got around to putting them in, she decided, staring at the clusters of exposed wires dotted along the walls. That or died trying.

The sheets on the immaculately made king-size bed were paper-thin, the embroidered cherry blossom motifs on the coverlet faded with age. But the lamp on the little half-circle table beside the bed was an antique bronze marvel, and the frame around the mirror could have encased a Renaissance masterpiece and not been out of place.

The bathroom was truly shudder-worthy: the towels grey with age, the bath stained an unhealthy shade of brown; no *way* was she getting in that bath.

A single white orchid sat in a fat crystal vase on the edge of the sink.

She laughed at that. At the eccentricity of it all and the outrageous potential of the place. Never mind that refurbishing the hotel wasn't a sensible option—not financially. She didn't need Ethan Hamilton's big black folder full of figures and calculations to tell her that. And still she closed her eyes and let herself dream.

Her project, not one of her father's soulless business acquisitions.

Hers alone.

Moments later her daydreaming came to an abrupt end at the sound of knocking. Not the water pipes, thankfully, just someone at the door. She left the bathroom and set forth across the ridiculously large room, thinking back to half-remembered art lessons about perfect proportions, perspective, and the illusion of space.

No illusions here. Just space, and the glimmer of a dream that wouldn't quite go away no matter how rational she tried to be. She shook her head, opened the door.

'Mr Ethan said to let you rest,' said Rajah, still resplendent in his turban and tunic. 'Whereas Ayah wanted to know if you were comfortable. Whom to obey was a most difficult decision.'

Mia stifled a smile. 'How did you decide?'

'I am not married to Mr Ethan.'

'Ah,' she said, and, because she couldn't help but be curious she asked, 'Is anyone married to Mr Ethan?'

'No, Miss Mia. His faithless wife is dead. Drowned at the hands of her evil lover, not two hundred yards from this very spot.'

Okey-dokey, then.

'Sadly, she haunts him still.'

'I can imagine. Er...you do mean that the *memory* of his wife haunts him, don't you? As opposed to the actual spectre?'

'Her form has never yet appeared in the hotel, Miss Mia. She is bound to the sea.'

Oh, good. Alice's Wonderland had *nothing* on this place. 'Does this mean the hotel has beachfront access?'

'But of course. We have our own beach. Have you not noticed it from your balcony?'

'I have a balcony?' Mia looked around the room. A trio of double-hung timber windows lined one wall, affording her a view of a vibrant, bustling city. The adjacent wall backed onto the hallway, where Rajah was standing. The doorway on the third side of the room led to the bathroom. Wood panelling covered the fourth wall. As for a balcony...

'Through the sitting room,' he said, and crossed the room to slide apart two of the wooden panels, and then another two, and then another two, until the entire wall peeled back to reveal a sun-drenched sitting room even larger than the bedroom—and, yes, a balcony, a thin strip of beach, and a view across the channel to Butterworth and beyond.

'Whoa.'

'Indeed so,' said Rajah. 'The Cornwallis Hotel commands a most advantageous location and exceptional views.'

If she stayed she'd need elocution lessons, never mind that English was her first language. She walked through into the sitting room, entranced by the light and spaciousness, the scent of the sea, and a waft of frangipani drifting in through the windows. 'Tell me, Rajah, how long have you been working here?'

'Sixty-three glorious years, Miss Mia.'

'And Ayah?'

'Sixty-one years.'

'How many people work here altogether?'

'Ten, in recent times.'

A skeleton staff, if that. 'How many in the hotel's heyday?'

'Seventy, including the elephant keepers.'

'We—ah—don't have any elephants in residence at the moment, do we?'

'No, Miss Mia. Your late grandfather, Mr Fletcher Senior, sent them to the zoo in 1959.'

'Oh, good.' Oh, God. 'I don't know if you can help me, Rajah, but I'd like you to try and find some old photographs of the hotel. I'd also like both you and Ayah to join me up here in about half an hour, for a briefing. I need to know how this place runs. Who does what and when. Who your clientele are. Who they used to be.' Mia smiled as the old man seemed to swell with pride and something that looked like a great deal like hope. 'You'd really love to see this place restored to its former glory, wouldn't you?'

Rajah smiled gently. 'Wouldn't you?'

* * *

By mid-morning the next day, Mia knew the worst of it. The hotel had belonged to her father's family for over a hundred years and had been in steady decline for the past fifty. Her father had started to resurrect it some twenty-five years ago but, according to Rajah, he'd lost heart. Lost it when he'd lost Lily. Those particular words had remained unspoken, but Mia had heard them anyway.

Following Mia's birth, her father had gifted Lily the hotel and headed for Australia, taking Mia with him. Now Lily had given it to her, probably as a way of giving it back to her father. A debt repaid. Nothing more. There was nothing for her here but echoes of a life she'd never known. Nothing but business. And still she continued to dream… To wonder what it would be like to be something other than immersed in Fletcher Corp business. No man had ever tempted her to detour, no passion for music or art or for a different career had ever made her deviate from the path her father had set her on. She liked the challenge of big business and always had.

But this old hotel… Her longing to know more about her mother… These things tempted her to swerve dangerously from the only road she'd ever known.

And stay a while.

Her father would have a fit. One of those calm, softly spoken, devastatingly cutting fits that flayed skin from bone. He didn't indulge in them often, people were smart enough not to encourage them, but if she stayed on…if she told him she wanted to restore the hotel and run it herself…Yep, her father would have a fit.

Maybe she'd know more after the reading of the will. Maybe that would help clarify her thoughts somewhat.

She could always hope.

By the time Ethan and the solicitor knocked on the door of her suite at midday Mia was ready for them. She'd dressed carefully in a pale blue cotton T-shirt, beige trousers, and sandals. She didn't look like the pampered daughter of a wealthy man. Nor did she look like a formidable businesswoman who'd cut her teeth on profit and loss statements. And that was exactly the way she wanted it. She didn't have to be either of those things here. She could be just Mia.

The notion was decidedly liberating.

'Mr Hamilton.'

Ethan's lips twitched. 'Miss Fletcher.' He introduced her to Bruce Tan, the solicitor who nodded and held out his hand.

Mia shook it. His hands were small, like her own, his clasp friendly and his eyes warmly curious, and she liked him all the better for him being upfront about it. *'Ni hao,'* she said. If she'd read the translation dictionary properly, it meant hello.

Ethan's eyes narrowed. 'I didn't know you spoke Mandarin.'

'My first word.' Mia smiled both at Ethan and at Bruce Tan. 'Come back tomorrow and I'll know another.'

'Why wait?' said Bruce Tan with a conspiratorial smile. *'Xie xie,* Miss Fletcher. That means thank you. So many visitors to our country never learn a word. Do you plan to stay long in Penang?'

Good question. 'To be perfectly honest, I have no

idea. My plans change by the minute. It's very disconcerting. I usually have more...'

'Focus?' supplied Ethan, with the hint of a smile.

'Direction,' she countered. 'Focus isn't usually a problem once I know what I want.' She stood back and motioned them inside. 'Come on through. I'm set up in the sitting room.'

Bruce Tan entered willingly, and after a strangely searching glance so did Ethan.

She settled Bruce in the king chair, a masterful touch that afforded him respect, before taking the seat to his left and positioning Ethan on *her* left so the solicitor could speak to them both without having to turn from one to the other. The financials Ethan had given her sat on the table within easy reach. A pitcher of water and an array of alcoholic beverages sat on the sideboard next to some glasses.

'How many people underestimate you?' murmured Ethan as he settled beside her.

'Everyone.' Mia shrugged. Such a small thing, the positioning of people at a table, but meetings had a way of progressing more smoothly when one paid attention to the little things. 'Blame it on my well-guided youth.'

She sat in silence as the solicitor ran through the terms of her mother's will. Everything was straightforward, just as Ethan had said. And all the while she listened to business a tiny part of her protested that this old hotel could be so much more than business if she let it.

Finally, the solicitor finished his spiel, and silence descended on the room. Her turn.

'Ethan gave me the profit and loss figures for the past three years,' she said, as she pulled the paperwork towards her. 'The hotel has lost significant amounts of money each year, yet there's no borrowing against capital and no accumulated debt.' She looked from the solicitor to Ethan. 'Who put in?'

'Lily's health was fading,' Ethan said curtly. 'She didn't need the worry of a hotel that wasn't breaking even, and she would never accept financial assistance from my father.'

'You cleared the debt?'

He nodded.

'Then you have claim on the hotel.'

'No.' His jaw tightened. 'You don't understand. You've known about my father and your mother—known about *me*—for a few days. I've known about you since I was six. The hotel's yours. It's always been yours. It's what Lily wanted.'

Mia sat ramrod straight as she digested his words. Not expecting them. Not knowing what to do with them. 'Thank you, Mr Tan,' she said at last. 'I think Ethan and I can take it from here.'

'A pleasure meeting you, Miss Fletcher. Enjoy your stay in Penang. I'll send a courier for the paperwork.' He rose from the table, nodded to Ethan, and left.

A charged silence settled over them once he was gone. The business end of the meeting was over; emotion ruled her now, swirling about her in waves she couldn't control. Anger, loss, confusion…

Hope.

'I realise you've hardly had time to consider all your options, but have you given any thought to what you'd like to do with the hotel?' asked Ethan finally.

She knew it was crazy, but the notion just wouldn't

go away. Maybe it was time she said it out loud. 'I've a mind to restore it.'

He eyed her steadily. 'You've seen the figures?'

'I've seen them.'

'Brave.'

'Foolish,' she corrected. 'Go ahead, say it. From a business perspective I should salvage what I can of the fittings and sell the rest for the price of the land. The problem is, I can *see* it,' she said softly. 'Everywhere I look I can see what this old place could be. What it *should* be.'

'What will your father say if you decide to restore it?'

'I don't know.' She rose from the table and walked to the balcony to stare out over the channel. Her father hadn't wanted her to come. He'd as good as instructed her to let their solicitors handle the sale of the hotel. But for once she'd defied him. She wanted answers, needed them desperately. And she would find them. 'I think I'm about to find out.'

The view, glorious as it was, didn't hold her attention. Ethan did. She watched in silence as he crossed to the counter, lined up two glasses, poured a generous shot of whisky into each and brought them over.

'Here. It'll help.'

Mia took the drink he held out to her, unprepared for the sudden fierce heat that rushed through her as their fingertips touched. She'd felt it yesterday when they'd shaken hands. She'd tried to tell herself she'd simply been hot, tired and overwrought; that her body had needed rest, that was all, and that after a decent night's sleep she'd be fine, just fine, beneath Ethan Hamilton's touch.

She'd been wrong.

Mia had been waiting for years to feel that quick rip of outrageous desire at a man's touch. Well, now she had.

With the son of the man her mother had run off with.

Dear Lord...please! Not him!

So what if he was tall, dark, and extremely well put together? She wasn't a pushover for a pretty package—never had been.

So what if there was a steadiness about him that spoke of strength and discipline, a spark that hinted at passion? She knew *dozens* of tall, dark, handsome, passionate men!

Okay, maybe not dozens. She knew maybe two, and it was a damn shame neither of them could conjure from her that fierce, shimmering awareness she felt when she looked into Ethan Hamilton's eyes.

Yes, Mia. Him.

She didn't sip her Scotch. She tossed it back, made a face, and swallowed hard.

So did he. 'More?'

'I think so.' He didn't hold out his hand for her glass. Instead he brought the bottle to her and poured another shot straight into it. She stared down at the amber liquid in the glass, not drinking it—not yet—trying to concentrate on business, on her mother, on anything and anyone but him. 'You've known about me since you were six?' she asked tentatively.

'Yes.' She thought that was the end of his answer, but then his eyes met hers, his expression resigned and surprisingly sympathetic. 'You're the sister who lived across the water,' he said quietly. 'The one who never came. But you are here now, and if you want my help

you have it. Protection, advice, finance, whatever…'
His lips tilted ever so slightly. 'I'm the big brother you
never knew you had.'

The *what?* She stared at him incredulously. Did he
seriously think she could treat him like a brother with
this need to touch him, taste him, so big inside her she
could hardly think straight? How on earth was she supposed to manage *that?*

He raised an eyebrow, as if waiting for her reply.

'Oh, good,' she said faintly, and downed her Scotch.

CHAPTER THREE

HE WASN'T bad for a brother she didn't want. They were back at the table, working through the refurbishment estimates, her mind firmly fixed on business, and Ethan was proving a remarkably good sounding board.

'Structural work first, including the electricals and the plumbing,' Mia said. 'Are these walls solid? Is that why the wiring and the pipes are on the outside?'

'They vary. Most of the plumbing is *ad hoc*. If you plan to hide the wiring and pipes you're looking at stripping the walls completely.'

'They'd have to be stripped and replastered anyway,' she countered. 'I mean, look at them. Maybe it won't cost that much more to make the pipes and wires disappear. Maybe it'll cost *less*.'

'This is going to cost you a fortune, Mia, and you know it.'

'I guess optimism isn't one of your strengths,' she said. 'That's okay. I have enough for both of us.'

'Uh-huh.'

'I can't wait to see a shine on all that marble.'

Ethan grinned, his features relaxed and unguarded, and all thoughts of kinship came to a screeching halt. His smile was downright lethal. Heart-stopping, in fact, because she was pretty sure hers just had.

'Will you close for renovations?'

Mia nodded. *Business, Mia, business. Ignore the smile.* 'The way I see it, I can do this agonisingly slowly, or boots 'n' all. I'm leaning heavily towards the latter.'

'You'll need a project manager.'

'I know. Architect or builder? Or both?'

'What sort of structural changes are you thinking of?'

'Hard to say until I've had a better look around. What I've seen so far I aim to keep. The spaces are superb.'

'Builder,' he said. 'One who specialises in restoration. I'll get a list to you tomorrow. We've dealt with some in the past.'

'This brother business is beginning to grow on me.' Pity about those decidedly unsisterly thoughts.

'What's your background, Mia Fletcher?' he said, still easy with her. 'What makes you think you can take on the Cornwallis Hotel and win?'

'Well, there's the business and marketing degree. That'll help.'

'Theoretically.'

'There's the fact that I've been working as my father's PA for the last three years.'

'That'll help more,' he said.

'More than you know,' she muttered.

'Which part of your father's business are you involved in, exactly?'

'All of it.'

'So you're being groomed to run the Fletcher corporation?'

'Maybe. Not necessarily. Probably not any time in the near future,' she admitted with a sigh. 'It's not that I don't understand the business. I do.'

'I don't doubt it,' he muttered, gesturing towards the papers in front of him.

'Unfortunately I'm not quite ruthless enough. Apparently it'll come with age, and getting worked over once too often.'

'Something to look forward to?'

'Yeah,' she said glumly.

'What will you do with the staff while you close for renovation?'

'I plan to bring Rajah and Ayah into the decision-making process. I'll be mining their memories, trying to find a way to incorporate the past into the new design. As for the others, they can work the same hours they work now. More if they choose to.'

'You're right.' He smiled again. 'You do have a problem with ruthlessness.'

'Yes, well, thanks for the vote of confidence. I plan to start them sorting and cleaning the fixtures I want to keep. The picture frames, the brass fittings, the chandelier...'

'Chandeliers,' he corrected. 'There's another one in the ballroom—a bigger one. And dozens of little ones.'

'I have a ballroom?' She jumped up from the table. 'I have a chandelier the size of a *helicopter*?'

'You're not heading for the Scotch again, are you?' he asked warily.

'Certainly not.' She *loved* this place. 'I'm heading for the ballroom.'

The ballroom enchanted her. Mia stood just inside the entrance doors with what she was pretty sure was a goofy smile on her face as she took in the unbridled opulence of the room. Sidelights—the smaller chandeliers Ethan had spoken of—adorned the walls, and the ceiling rose in steps to frame a masterpiece of dripping, swooping, looping crystal. Beneath the dust on the floor lay wooden parquetry, a football field of parquetry, in various shades of brown. She leaned closer, noticing the different grains in the different coloured woods. 'It's not all one type of wood stained different colours, is it?'

'No. It's rosewood, red oak, ebony and beech.'

'Whoa.' The floor was divine. 'What's behind those doors at the far end?'

'The elephant walkway.'

Mia slid him a sideways glance.

'I'm serious,' he said.

'And after that?'

'The ocean.'

She believed him. But she had to see it for herself. The doors opened out onto a smallish concrete platform. Cut into the ground below them was a narrow walkway that ran the length of the building and disappeared around each of the corners. 'People used to come to the ball by *elephant?*'

'Not really—although I expect they could have if they'd wanted to. Mostly the keepers used the walk to take the elephants to and from the beach, and this landing to wash them down with fresh water afterwards. Ask Rajah to find you the photos of the keepers standing up here, scrubbing them down with brooms.'

Mia grinned, already imagining wall plaques and photos explaining to the guests of today the history of the elephants of the past. She could bridge the walkway so people could look down on it from above. Put stairs to one side so they could walk down into it and view more plaques and more photos of yesteryear. She'd run a tropical garden from the bridge all the way down to the beach. Weave a walkway through it that led back round to the stairs. She could see it now. 'I'll need a landscape architect.'

'I'll get you a list.'

'Do I have a gardener at the moment?'

'You have Rajah, who waters the planter boxes out the front.'

She'd need a gardener as well. Later. She turned to ask Ethan about that, too, but he chose that moment to smile his rakish, thoroughly amused smile, and the words died on her lips. Shared amusement was all well and good. Until it deepened and blurred into something far more elemental. 'I…ah…' She'd forgotten her train of thought. There was only heat and need. Such a terrifying need to touch him.

'We can interview for groundsmen,' he said, picking up the unspoken thread of the conversation. 'When you're ready for them.'

'Yes.' She tried to follow his lead, tried to concentrate on the business at hand, but her body betrayed her. She swayed towards him, buffeted by an unseen wind, and his hand shot out to steady her, only to stop at the last minute, just before he touched her.

'Have you had lunch?' he asked gruffly.

'Not yet.'

'You need food. Next time I offer you Scotch I'm doing it after you've eaten.'

He ushered her back into the ballroom, shutting the landing door behind them, and their footsteps echoed hollowly through the room as they crossed the floor. The doors at the far end were massive, with long brass handles that she and Ethan reached for at the same time. There was room enough for two hands along the length of the handle, room enough for four, and still their hands collided.

The jolt was stronger this time, fiercer, and Mia cursed beneath her breath even as she jerked her hand away.

'Allow me,' said Ethan tightly.

'Thank you.' *Damn you.*

Time to get the hell out of the ballroom.

Ethan took her to a bustling open-air pavilion by the beach, not far from the hotel, for lunch. He came here a lot, decided Mia as the waiters greeted him with easy familiarity, and judging by the surreptitious glances in her direction, and the fast and furious whispers that followed, her mother had been a frequent customer, too. An older man rushed out of the kitchen to greet them— the chef, perhaps, or possibly the restaurant owner. He embraced Ethan and launched into rapid conversation. Not English, Malay or Mandarin, she decided after a moment. Possibly Tamil.

'Joh, this is Mia,' said Ethan, catching her eye and switching smoothly to English. 'Lily's daughter.'

'What? You think I don't have eyes?' the older man said. 'Why you not give me more notice? You think I can prepare a feast in five minutes? Come back in two hours and we shall honour your mother properly.'

'Well, we *could*,' said Ethan doubtfully. 'But we've just read the will, and I think food will help. I forgot about Mia's jet lag. Then there's the heat…the…'

'Emotion,' she supplied helpfully.

'Exactly. I gave her Scotch on an empty stomach.' He eyed her accusingly. 'She sways.'

Swoon. Sway. No need to argue technicalities. 'Food *would* help.'

Their host agreed. Not only did they get the shadiest table in the pavilion, along with iced water and a bowl of spiced peanuts to nibble on, he demanded they order immediately for the sake of her health. The problem was she had no idea what to choose.

'Perhaps the Nonya fish with steamed greens?' he suggested.

'Lovely.' Mia closed her menu and handed it to him. Ethan ordered a mixed seafood dish and Joh retreated to the kitchen, barking orders as he went.

'What did I just order?'

'Whole fish covered with a Portugese mix of herbs and spices and baked in a clay oven. Very rich. Very delicate. I think you'll like it. Your mother loved it.'

Your mother.

'Can we not call her that?' said awkwardly. It's just…' Mia shrugged. 'Can we just call her Lily?'

'If that's what you want.'

That was the trouble. She didn't know what she wanted.

'You can ask me about her if you like,' he offered after a moment.

'No.' Finally something she was sure of. She wouldn't get the answers she sought from Ethan. 'I have a feeling you'd tell me she was kind and loving and wonderful, and I'd hate you for it. My father never remarried, Ethan. I could have done with a mother, even one who lived half a world away. You got her. I didn't.' She eyed him darkly. 'Bastard.'

Ethan blinked. 'You're *jealous* of me?'

'Of course I am. Haven't you ever heard of sibling rivalry?'

'Well...yes. I've just never had to deal with it.'

'Hey, you're the one who wanted a sister. May I ask you a personal question?'

'Is *no* an option?'

'What do you wear when you're not wearing a suit?' She sat back and waved a hand in the general direction of his charcoal-grey suit. 'You look outstanding in them, by the way, but what do you wear on your days off?'

'Morning or evening?'

Mia rolled her eyes. 'Both.'

'Well, nothing to begin with, then a towel, then boxers, then trousers—'

Mia was enjoying the visual just a little too much. 'Perfectly pressed or casually creased?'

'Something wrong with ironing?'

'Not if you do it yourself.'

'Housekeeping does the ironing,' he said. 'Have you finished interrupting?'

Mia nodded.

'Then a shirt. A casual, comfortable, uncreased shirt.'

'With a collar?'

'Yes, but no tie. I might even leave the top button undone. Sometimes two. But only after a big night.'

'Do you *ever* get dishevelled?'

His eyes gleamed. 'Occasionally. Would you like me to describe what I'd be wearing then? It won't take long.'

'No,' she said hastily. Her imagination was already

there. And, because she couldn't help it, 'Does your hair get all mussed up and spiky?'

'Only if someone's fists are in it.'

Mia let out her breath in a hurry as the heat beneath the canopy seemed to build. 'Phew. Hot in here isn't it?'

'It is now.' A smile tugged at his lips. 'What do you want to know, Mia? Whether there's more to me than just a suit or whether there's someone I undress for on a regular basis?'

'Well…ah…as your sister I should probably know both.'

'Yes,' he said. 'And no.'

'You mean yes to being complex and interesting and no to being attached? Or are you currently undecided on both questions?' He was grinning outright now; his smile crooked and his eyes amused. 'I have this really strong urge to thump you,' she muttered. 'It must be a sisterly impulse.'

'Hold that thought,' he said. 'Cleave to it.'

'You haven't answered the question, Ethan.'

She didn't think he was going to. His smile faded and his eyes hardened. 'I was married once. These days I prefer something far less permanent. There's no one you need know about. What about you?' he asked abruptly. 'Is there anyone waiting for you back in Australia?'

'No. I've been…' What? *Searching for a man who can make me feel the way you do?* That'd go down well. 'Busy with other things,' she said with a shrug. 'Don't get me wrong. I love the idea of a family of my own, a husband to love and babies to cherish. But first I need to fall in love.'

'You've never been in love?'

'Not yet. Although I do occasionally fall into lust.'

Ethan's eyes narrowed. 'Define *occasionally.*'

'Every now and then,' she said, readily enough. 'You're not going all brotherly on me, are you? I'm twenty-four years old, Ethan. I'm not a—'

'Don't say it!' he interrupted hurriedly. 'Not another word. God, where's the food?'

Mia grinned. 'What else would you like to know?'

'Nothing. Absolutely nothing! My admiration for men with sisters has just risen immeasurably. It's a whole new world.'

Mia eased back into her chair and looked around her at the colourful clothing and unfamiliar faces of the people around her. The scent of fresh fish and exotic spices teased at her senses, and voices filled her ears with new sounds and inflections. Everything was so very, very different from the world she'd left behind. 'Isn't it just?'

Knowledge was the key to understanding, decided Mia later that afternoon, as she stood at the door to her parents' residential quarters on the third and top floor of the hotel's north wing. They'd lived here before she was born. Her mother, according to Rajah, had used it as her day base for many years after. Lily had a connection to the place, he'd told her. One that couldn't be broken.

It was only natural she feel some apprehension as she stepped through the door—alone, in spite of Rajah and Ayah's vigorous protests that someone accompany her. She was used to being alone and here, at the start of it all, she needed to be.

Her first impression was one of darkness and gloom, but maybe that was due more to all the shades being drawn than the actual décor. Mia made her way from window to window, drawing shades aside as she went, until the rooms were bathed in sunlight, and then she turned around and looked again. And smiled.

Her mother had loved colour and texture and had used both abundantly. Jewel-hued silk cushions vied for attention against lounge chairs of purple and cream striped velvet. Rugs of emerald-green and midnight-blue covered the floor. Everywhere she looked she saw rich strokes of colour that should have clashed but didn't, and through it all, mirroring the hotel rooms below, ran an eclectic mixture of the shabby and the exquisite.

Lily had been fond of chess, if the elegant board and pewter pieces set for play between two deep and comfortable-looking chairs were any indication. Fond of photography, too, if the photos on the wall were any indication. Asian streetscapes, bustling and lively, jostled for wall space alongside close-ups of different faces of different races—all of which, Mia suspected, could be found in Penang.

She stood for a long time in front of a photograph of her father, covered in mud and laughing, really laughing, shovel in hand as he tried to stop a section of bank from sliding into what looked suspiciously like the elephant walkway. Had her mother been the photographer? Had they both been laughing as she'd taken the shot?

There were pictures of Ethan as a child; it had to be him. Pictures of Ethan and a tall handsome man with a warm smile and eyes that held a hint of sadness—Ethan's father, most likely. But the most intriguing photo of all was a distant shot of two men and a boy fishing from a beach. Her father was one of the men. Ethan was the boy. The other man was Ethan's father. They'd known one another then, these two men. Once upon a time they'd been friends.

Had her mother taken that photograph, too? Had she taken them all?

Was that why she never appeared *in* any of them?

Mia had come here looking for answers. She'd wanted to know what type of woman her mother was, what type of woman could walk away from her husband and newborn baby and never look back. But there were no answers in these photographs. Just moments frozen in time, moments special to her mother, and they only raised more questions.

Why had her mother stopped loving her father? Why had Ethan's father fallen in love with someone else's wife? How did people get it so wrong?

Didn't they care who they hurt?

Turning her back on the pictures, Mia headed unseeingly for the door. She couldn't do this right now. She'd explore her mother's rooms and belongings later.

Ethan found his father at his home on the other side of the island, watering orchids on the balcony that eased out from the kitchen. He watched in silence, absorbing the changes the house had seen since Lily's death. For the first time ever there were no half-read books scattered about, no flowers in the vase on the kitchen table. He missed the lived-in look, missed the fragrance of the flowers, their colour and their warmth. The house felt colder without Lily in it. Emptier.

Loneliness had moved in.

'I don't know how much water to give them,' said

Nathaniel Hamilton gruffly as he turned off the hose.
'I dare say that's enough.'

Water dripped from hanging baskets and ran in rivu-
lets over the tiles. 'I dare say you're right,' agreed Ethan,
relieved to see a whisper of humour beneath the shadows in his father's eyes.

'You read through the will with Mia today?' asked
his father after a moment's hesitation. 'You've seen
her?'

'Yeah.' Telling his father he'd made a complete hash
of welcoming her to the family was never going to be
easy. Telling him he wanted to haul her into his arms
and devour her was downright impossible.

'And?'

Ethan shrugged and ran a hand through his hair.
'She's independent, wary, and perfectly capable of sell-
ing, managing, or restoring the hotel without assistance.
She knows business. Richard's taught her well.'

His father eyed him speculatively. 'You extended my
invitation?'

'Yes.'

'And the broader one?'

'That, too. Right now she doesn't want anything to
do with us. Until a few days ago she thought her mother
had died twenty-four years ago. Whose idea was *that?*'

'Not mine,' snapped his father. 'It was something
Richard and Lily agreed on.'

'She's hurting. She wants answers.'

Nathaniel turned away, suddenly old and far frailer
than Ethan had ever seen him. 'Richard loved Lily with
everything he had,' his father said quietly. 'So did I.
And Lily, in her own way, loved us both. She chose us.

Richard had no one. He granted her her freedom and took Mia in return. It had a certain symmetry to it.'

Ethan scowled. The memory of Mia's haunted grey eyes, of her confusion when she spoke of her mother and of inheriting the hotel whispered through his brain, and he was suddenly very, very angry with Richard, Lily, *and* his father. 'Tell me,' he said scathingly, 'did any of you ever stop to think of *Mia?*'

'People make mistakes, Ethan,' said his father wearily. 'Mistakes they deeply regret. You know that better than anyone. If we're lucky, we get the opportunity to atone for them before we die.'

Ethan said nothing. His father was right.

'I want her to know how much her mother loved her. I want to give her that much, even if she takes nothing else from us. I need you to keep trying to reach her. Please.'

He didn't want to. Not with Mia on his mind and a hunger he didn't know how to control echoing through his brain. But there was nothing else he could do. 'All right,' he muttered. 'All right, I'll try.'

His father hesitated. 'Ethan…? What's she like?'

Now it was Ethan's turn to hesitate as he looked out over the magical gardens his father had spent a fortune creating: a peaceful sanctuary fashioned to soothe even the most tortured of souls. He would find no solace here today.

'Breathtaking.'

CHAPTER FOUR

'MR ETHAN to see you, Miss Mia,' announced Rajah.

Mia looked up from the restoration quotes scattered across the desk of what had formerly been the guest library but had since become her office. 'Thanks, Rajah.'

Rajah disappeared, Ethan stayed, and Mia's heart skipped a beat. A week had passed since their lunch date. A week in which she'd almost convinced herself that her outrageous desire to get naked with him had been due to the reading of the will and her heightened emotional state at the time. But…no.

One look at him standing in the doorway, so calm and watchful, and that particular notion died a glorious and speedy death. She still wanted him just as much as she had before. Maybe more.

'Nice suit,' she said, and his eyes warmed, just a little, before his control kicked in and his mask of formality slid smoothly back into place.

'How are you, Mia?'

'Busy.' She couldn't shake his hand the way a business acquaintance would, and had no hope whatsoever of pulling off a sisterly greeting. Five minutes. She figured that was all they had before her urge to touch him got the better of her. 'Social visit, is it?'

'Business. One of your tenders came to my hotel by mistake.'

'You should have called. I'd have sent someone over for it.'

'Yeah, but then I wouldn't have had even the faintest chance of taking a look at it.'

'You think you have one now?'

'I'm hoping so.' He held up a large envelope and slid it onto her desk. 'Have any others come in?'

'All but one.' She'd been looking them over before he arrived, and truth be told she could use another set of eyes. Someone who knew Penang and its people. Someone who knew whether Chinese electrical contractors could work with Indian plumbers and Indonesian plasterers. Someone who could tell her straight whether all of them, or none of them, would take direction from *her*. 'Is that the Kwong tender?'

He nodded. 'Am I going to have to beg?'

She had a very brief, very erotic vision of Ethan on his knees in front of her, with his hair all mussed on account of her hands being in it, but he wasn't the one doing the begging.

She was.

'As it turns out, I need a second opinion,' she said with a sigh. 'It may as well be yours.' There was no getting round the fact that good business often required huge personal sacrifice. 'No begging required.'

'Well,' he said with a grin as he pulled up a chair. 'That's a relief.'

Cobbling together a workforce of fifty or so tradesmen, craftsmen and labourers wasn't easy—even with Ethan's help. The Kwong tender could supply the electricians, plumbers, and plasterers they needed, along with a substantial labour force. The Samsul contingent could provide the craftsmen.

There was a lot to be said for hiring them both.

'Which still leaves me in need of a project manager.' None of the men on the list Ethan had given her were available for months. 'Could *I* take it on?'

'No. Your gender will be a problem here, Mia. So will your youth.'

She'd figured as much. 'Who, then? I don't suppose you know any retired property developers looking for a project to take on? Someone with hefty local knowledge and a willingness to put the hotel's best interests at heart?'

Ethan sat back and surveyed her intently. 'Do you really want me to give you an answer?'

'Why wouldn't I?'

'You could always ask my father.'

Oh. That was why.

'He's retired, experienced, and guaranteed to put your interests first.'

'No.'

'He could use the distraction, Mia. Lily's death hit him hard. He's grieving.'

'No!'

'You said you wanted answers.'

'Don't you know when to stop?' she demanded.

'He's not to blame,' said Ethan curtly.

'He stole another man's wife and denied me a mother! Why shouldn't I blame him? Tell me, Ethan, are you this forgiving of *your* late wife's lover?'

'No.' One word filled with menace and interlaced with anguish.

Not forgiven, she thought with a shudder, and knew

instinctively that she should never have prodded at that particular wound. 'Then don't ask it of me,' she muttered.

'The way I heard it, Lily asked for a divorce. Your father agreed, but his price was high. If he couldn't have Lily then she couldn't have you.'

'No.' Mia shook her head vehemently. She didn't believe him.

'An eye for an eye, Mia.'

No. 'My father wouldn't do that. He's not like that. It was *your* father who didn't want me.'

'My father would have welcomed you in a heartbeat. You could have stayed with Richard and come to us for visits. He'd have welcomed *any* contact with you whatsoever. He still would, if you'd let him.'

'You're lying!'

'You only wish I was.' Ethan's gaze seared her, flayed her. She heard the truth in his words. She'd have given anything not to hear it. 'Mia—'

'I don't want to hear it! What kind of father denies his child a mother? What kind of mother lets him?'

'Mia—'

'No!' she screamed as her control deserted her. Emotion ruled her now, and its colour was red. 'Leave me alone!'

Lily's quarters were an unlikely refuge, but Mia didn't go there seeking solace. She went there to give her anger direction.

'Who were you?' she raged at her unseen mother. 'How could you?' She halted in front of the photo of her father, all the fight going out of her. 'How could *you?*'

For all his faults, his stern and distant ways, she

loved him—still loved him. 'How could you get love so *wrong?*'

She turned her back on that beloved, smiling face and slumped against the wall below it, sliding down until she was sitting on the floor, with her back to the wall and her knees to her chest, willing the pain to go away. She wanted to be as untouchable as the porcelain dolls in the cabinet next to her. Locked away from the world and safe from harm.

She tried to lock herself away, tried to be strong. But the blows had gone too deep, hammering at the heart of her. As it was she settled for resting her cheek on her knees and focussing on the dolls in the cabinet instead. The sleeping baby doll, her tiny fist curled tight against the world as she slept. The toddler, her frilly nappy-clad bottom high in the air as she bent over and peeked between her chubby knees with a two-toothed grin on her face. Porcelain they might be but the doll maker had managed to capture the essence of a little girl.

Haltingly, Mia tried the cabinet door. Not locked away at all. There were other dolls. Playful, friendly little cherubs, and delicate little girls, and exquisitely beautiful young women almost too fragile and too perfect to touch.

She reached for the topmost doll—the sleeping baby, with lashes so fine and cheeks so perfectly coloured she couldn't help but brush a finger against them—and set it in her lap. The porcelain was smooth and cool to the touch, the tiny linen shirt soft and fine against her fingertips. She saw writing on the hem of the shirt and turned it over, expecting to find the name of the doll maker written there, or perhaps even the name of the doll. But the ink had blurred and she could barely make out that there were two distinct words.

'It says "Happy Birthday",' said Ethan from above her, and she looked up to find him standing beside her, his hands at his side and his expression unfathomable. 'This one's my favourite.' He gestured towards the peek-a-boo toddler. 'I helped choose her. Mind you, I was seven at the time. I probably thought she was funny.'

'She is,' she said softly, and then, with more strength, 'I'm sorry, Ethan. I shouldn't have gotten so angry with you. Whatever happened back then between the three of them…it's not your fault.'

'She used to have the catalogues sent from England,' he said, as if he hadn't even heard her. 'She'd leaf through them for weeks before making her final decision. The dolls always arrived the last week of June, and went into the cabinet on the second of July.'

Mia stared at him, the doll in her hands forgotten. She knew that date well.

'There's twenty-four of them,' he said quietly. 'Happy Birthday, Mia.'

Ethan knew that Mia was smart, savvy, and clear-headed when it came to business. She'd proven it downstairs as they'd gone over the tenders. Rajah had told him she was generous with the staff, and receptive to their ideas without being a pushover. But right now, kneeling in front of a cabinet full of dolls, she came undone.

So fragile. He could see the delicate outline of her shoulder blades as she sat there hunched over a doll, with her head bowed and a curtain of straight black hair shielding her face. She was trembling, he saw with dismay, and then, as he knelt down to brush her hair back from her face, he saw the tears tracking down her cheeks.

'Oh, hell!' he muttered. 'I don't pretend to understand what happened, but she loved you, Mia. She never forgot you. Not for one day.'

Her tears started in earnest then, and he couldn't stand it. 'Don't,' he said, prising the doll from her hands and setting it gently aside, before pulling her up and drawing her into his arms. So broken, he thought. So alone.

He meant to comfort, nothing more. To offer his strength because hers had run out. But her scent wrapped around him, whispering through his memory and finding purchase there. Familiar. Her hands fisted against his chest and his hands in her hair. The softness of her hair and the curve of her cheek. The fine tremors that rocked her as she rode out her anger and her grief. All of it uncomprehendingly, inescapably familiar.

'Shh,' he murmured, when the worst of it was over, and felt a fist thump against his chest—not hard, but hard enough to feel it.

'Don't you shush me, Ethan Hamilton,' she said in a choked voice.

'Sorry. My mistake.' Women! 'You just let it all out.'

Another thump and a strangled laugh as he ran a hand down her spine, wondering just how the hell such a small sound could shatter a man's defences so completely.

'Enough with the soothing!' Her fists unclenched momentarily, and when they clenched again the material of his shirt was in them. His hands slid down her back and curved around her waist, automatically doing what hands did when a body wanted more. How the hell did she come to be in his arms? He couldn't remember.

Oh, yeah. A tremor racked him as her hands brushed his nipples. Comfort.

He'd pray for mercy if he thought it would help. Or if he thought he deserved it.

As it was, he prayed for the strength to let her go. 'So...we're done here,' he said trying to make his voice sound a little less husky and a lot more businesslike. 'You know, with the tears?'

'All done,' she said shakily. 'You're...ah...probably wondering if you can let go of me now. You can.'

He couldn't. 'Maybe if you just pulled free...' His hands tightened around her waist as he said it. *Her* hands were smoothing the tiny creases she'd made from his shirt and sending the skin beneath into ecstasy. 'That'd work.' Theoretically.

But she didn't.

And neither did he. There were a million reasons why she shouldn't be in his arms. He'd sworn an oath to Lily to protect her, to treat her like a sister. Sworn a similar oath to his father. He didn't want to hurt her. Damn sure he didn't want to be attracted to her.

But he was.

He couldn't seem to drag his gaze away from her lips.

'Ethan...' She sounded breathless, needy. He loved the sound of his name on her lips. 'Ethan, we shouldn't do this. This is a really bad idea.'

'I know,' he muttered, and set his lips to hers.

One touch.

That was all it took and Mia was lost. His taste was dark and cool. Dangerously arousing, impossibly perfect, assaulting her senses, conjuring up memories that never were and never had been. Here… Now… At last. Everything she'd been seeking. Everything and more. Her hands fisted in his shirt and she made a tiny sound in her throat, a wordless plea for more. And he heard it. Gave it. Moving fast as he pressed her against the wall, his hands snaking into her hair as his lips crushed down on hers.

Mia's heart faltered and her breath left her body as Ethan poured into her. Outrageous desire, overwhelming need, and she let them come, embracing them as she opened her mouth to his onslaught and yielded.

She always yielded.

And the flames around them licked higher, dazzling and deadly, engulfing them both.

Ethan couldn't get enough of her. He'd never get enough. The thought slammed into him, terrified him, and gave him the strength to drag his hands from her hair and step away. He had to—someone had to—because if they didn't end this now he'd never let her go.

He stood there, breathing hard as Mia continued to lean against the wall, watching him with those luminous grey eyes that promised heaven as well as the depths of hell. Waiting…knowing…the same way he knew that if he reached for her again they'd both burn.

'Well,' she said raggedly. 'That certainly seemed to…work.' She picked up the porcelain baby and set her gently back in the cabinet, with her cheek to the glass and her hand to her heart, and shut the door.

'We shouldn't do that again,' he muttered.

'Agreed.'

'I promised your mother I'd look out for you. I promised *myself* I'd treat you like a sister.'

'Yeah, well, good luck with that.' Her voice gathered strength as she turned back towards him. 'Fortunately the thought of my father's reaction if I ever...if we ever...' She smoothed her hair back behind her ear with nervous fingers. 'Well, let's just say it's a deterrent. A big one.'

'Good,' he said. 'Good. I like it.'

'Feel free to borrow it,' she said somewhat dryly.

'No, you keep it,' he said. 'I have more than enough deterrents of my own.'

Ethan made it back to his hotel, back to his office, before allowing himself to think about Mia. Not about kissing her, mind—he was trying very hard not to think about that at all—but about her need for a project manager and the promise he'd made to Lily to protect her. He didn't doubt her business acumen, she had it in spades, but she'd never done business in Penang, and *that* would make all the difference. She *needed* someone with experience to head up this project. Someone who'd put the needs of the old hotel first. Someone who'd do his best to protect her interests.

Someone like him.

He could do it. He looked over his schedule for the coming months and ran a hand around the back of his neck. Okay, so maybe he'd need some help. His father would have to come out of retirement and pick up the reins of the Hamilton Group business again. But that wasn't necessarily a bad thing. Nathaniel would do it. He'd do it for Mia, and in doing so would have something to occupy his days while he settled to life without Lily.

Satisfied that the idea was sound, Ethan reached for

the phone and started making calls. The first was to his father, who agreed to his proposal with encouraging enthusiasm.

The next one was to Mia.

'I have a solution,' he said, when she answered the phone.

'I'm glad to hear it.' She sounded amused. Recovered. This was a good thing. 'To what?'

'You can project manage through me until someone becomes available.'

'Ethan—'

He'd expected her to hesitate—prepared for it. 'C'mon, Mia—you need a front man. I'm offering local knowledge, experience as a hotelier and developer, *and* I have an obligation to protect you. This is a win-win offer.'

'What about your own work?'

'It's covered.'

'Do you really think we can work together?' she said, after a long, long pause.

'What happened this morning won't happen again,' he said firmly. 'We were fine until we stopped talking business. Better than fine. We worked well together. You know we did.'

'So…we ban any talk of family?' she said dubiously.

'Exactly. Business all the way. And no more tears. Tears are bad.'

'Am I allowed frustration?' she asked dryly.

'Certainly. Sarcasm, too.'

'What about anger?'

'Whose?' He couldn't see her reluctant smile. He was staring out of his office window. But he felt it.

'Ethan—' she said, and stopped as if choosing her

words carefully. 'I know you feel some sort of family obligation towards me, but I'm not your responsibility.'

'You're talking family again,' he warned.

'My lack of a project manager is not your responsibility.'

'Better.'

'You'd be my last resort, Ethan.'

'As long as you have one.'

'I've been contemplating another solution,' she said awkwardly. 'Another possible project manager. He's almost as qualified as you, give or take some outdated local knowledge.'

He thought he knew who she was talking about.

'I'm thinking of asking my father.'

'When are you coming home?' Richard Fletcher spoke curtly, impatiently, and Mia ran nervous fingers through her hair. She needed a project manager, that much was true, but more than that she needed her father's blessing.

'That depends,' she hedged. 'Is this a bad time to call?'

'I'm having dinner with a client in fifteen minutes,' he said. 'You can have five of them.'

She closed her eyes and pictured him in his apartment, getting ready for yet another evening of business. She missed him, missed talking to him, but it was disconcerting just how much she didn't miss the business.

'I'm thinking of restoring the hotel,' she said baldly.

'You mean there's restoration work already in progress that you'll finish up before you sell?'

'No, Daddy. I mean the Cornwallis is exactly as you left it, only twenty-four years worse for wear. I want to restore it. Run it. Keep it.'

'You should reconsider,' he said after a long, long pause. 'You'll never make your money back.'

'This isn't about money.'

'It's always about money,' he corrected curtly. 'And, while we're on the subject, how do you think you're going to bankroll this renovation?'

'I'll use my trust fund. My portfolio.'

'That's insane. You can sell everything you own, Mia, and you'll still come up short. Trust me.'

'I do trust you, Daddy. For twenty-four years you told me my mother was dead when she wasn't, and I *still* trust you.'

Silence. Then, 'What do you want from me?'

'Your blessing,' she said quietly. 'Your help.'

'I'm more than happy to help you sell it.'

'Guess where I am now?'

'I don't have time for games, Mia.'

He never did. 'I'm in a ballroom with a chandelier made out of ten thousand pieces of hand-cut Austrian crystal. Late-afternoon sun is filtering in through a dozen arched windows, painting patterns on a floor made out of rosewood, beech, ebony and oak. Do you know where I'm standing, Daddy?'

Silence.

'The subcontractors are in place. Builders, craftsmen, labourers. Ethan's been helping me. You remember Ethan?'

'Come home.' Her father sounded nothing like his usual self. He sounded old, defeated.

'I need a project manager. Someone who believes in this place…in what it could be. You believed in it once. I've seen pictures of you.'

'Don't ask it of me, Mia.'

'I'm trying very hard to forgive her, Daddy. Forgive you.'

'You're asking the impossible. There's nothing for me there. Nothing for you.'

Mia stopped pacing to stare around the vast and empty ballroom. Sunlight streamed in through the windows, turning the dust she'd kicked up into dancers. 'You're wrong.'

At exactly three minutes past nine the following morning, Mia walked into the foyer of the Hamilton Hotel. She hadn't realised that it was less than three blocks away from the Cornwallis Hotel—hadn't realised it was one of the best and biggest luxury resorts on the island. No chandelier, though, she thought somewhat smugly. Just bold use of oriental colours, clever lighting, and decidedly unusual artwork.

Gathering her composure, and surreptitiously checking her appearance in the thoughtfully placed mirror, Mia straightened the collar on her crisp pink linen shirt, and headed for the reception desk.

She wasn't even sure Ethan would be in.

She should have called and made an appointment, or better still discussed it over the phone, she told herself for the hundredth time. But she needed to know if she could be in the same room as him and still concentrate on business. If she couldn't, there was no point broaching the subject at all. She'd thank him politely for his time, tell him she planned to advertise locally and in Australia for a project manager, and be on her way. Problem solved. Sort of.

The woman at Reception smiled politely and reached

for the phone when she asked for Ethan. 'I'll let him know, Ms...?'

'Fletcher,' supplied Mia.

'Ms Fletcher to see you, sir.' Beautiful phone voice. Beautiful manners. Excellent eye contact.

'Mr Hamilton would like to know if you'd prefer him to meet you downstairs or if you'd rather go on up.'

'I...ah...up where?'

The woman smiled again and silently handed Mia the phone, before moving away and making herself busy out of earshot.

'Your receptionist is very, very good,' Mia said into the phone. 'I'll need one of those, too, eventually. How much are you paying her?'

'More than you.' Ethan sounded amused. 'I'm in my apartment—top floor. I have an office up here, a kitchen and dining room, a couple of living areas, and a bed.'

'Can you *see* the bed from the office?'

'No.'

'I'll come up.'

'Good. You'll enjoy the view.'

'You...ah...are dressed, aren't you?' No way was she venturing into his apartment if he'd just rolled out of bed. That particular view she wanted to avoid.

'It's a charcoal-grey pinstripe. Single-breasted. You'll like it.'

She heard the smile in his voice, cursed herself for reacting to it. 'Oh, good,' she said, and hung up.

Ethan's penthouse was as sophisticated and enigmatic as the man himself. Luxury was a given, but there were homier touches around the place, too. She thought she saw Lily's influence in the boldly coloured wall tapes-

try depicting a Chinese battle scene, and in the photos
of the various Hamilton hotels hanging on the wall. The
furnishings were a deep, rich blue, very masculine, and
doubtless wickedly comfortable, but a battered wooden
sea chest with his name carved on it in a childish hand
spoke of a willingness to take his past with him into
the present. She liked that about him—that he valued
the journey as well as the destination.

He was right about the view. She did enjoy it. And
the floor-to-ceiling windows on three sides of the enormous living room showcased it superbly.

'That's the Padang,' he said, of a central square
of green far below them. 'To the west of the playing
field is City Hall, to the south the Victoria Memorial
Clocktower. Look out the windows to your left and
you'll see Chinatown; look behind you and you'll see
Little India.'

So much to know, she thought. So much to see.
'Thank you for seeing me at such short notice.'

'Did you call your father?' he asked quietly.

'Yes.' So he'd gathered the reason for her visit. There
was no point mincing words. 'He said no.'

Ethan said nothing.

'I was wondering,' she said carefully, 'what you
charge for your project management services.'

'There's no charge, Mia.'

'Because you're a philanthropist?'

'No.'

His lips twitched, and Mia hastily averted her gaze
and tried to think of business.

'I'll try and do as much of it as I can. If you could
just be an authoritative presence at the start...' she said,
staring past the playing field to the water beyond. 'And

if anything comes up that needs troubleshooting...'
Which, given the complexities and the age of the hotel,
was bound to be practically everything. 'Oh, hell. I'm
asking too much of you, aren't I?' She turned back towards him anxiously. 'What about your own work?'

'I've got it covered.'

'Yes, but you shouldn't have to.'

'I'm a trained architect, Mia. One of the reasons we
have so many hotels is because I keep designing and
building them. We don't *need* any more. Not for quite
some time. So here I am. Offering to help you renovate
the Cornwallis for several reasons—not all of which are
altruistic. You're not the only one who sees it as it was,
Mia. As it could be.'

'So you'll do it?' she said.

He nodded.

'And we'll keep our association strictly business?'

'Business all the way,' he said.

'I'm usually more careful,' she muttered, worrying at
her lower lip. 'I've always been a very rational person.'
Her father had taught her better than to mix business
with emotions, but hers were firmly tied up with this
old hotel. She didn't just *want* to fix it, she *needed* to
fix it—as if by doing so she could somehow find what
she'd been missing. A connection to Lily, maybe, or
just a different life from the one mapped out for her at
Fletcher Corp. Whatever it was, she knew with bone-
deep certainty that the hotel was the key. 'And then I
came here.'

And discovered a side of herself she hadn't even
known existed.

'So it's settled, then?' he said, with the hint of a smile.

'Yes. Caution appears to be taking a holiday.' In more

ways than one. 'If you want in, you're in. I'll need a couple of days to pull the finance together. We could set up a meeting with the contractors any time after that.'

'You want to meet with them here or at the Cornwallis?'

'There, I think. It'll be easier to walk them through it if we're there.'

Ethan nodded. 'Will you know what you want by then?'

'It's in my head, Ethan, and it's blindingly clear.'

'Well…this is a good thing,' he said, keeping his voice carefully neutral. 'But is it feasible?'

'Oh, the voice of reason?' She grinned. She couldn't help it. 'That *will* come in handy.'

'Now you're just trying to scare me.'

'So…nine a.m. Friday?'

'I'll be there.'

Mia hesitated, but only for a moment. 'I'm guessing that a boy who roamed the Cornwallis as a child and grew up to be an architect would have a fair few drawings tucked away. Dreams of what it could be. What he wanted it to be. No promises, mind, but I'm not completely closed to suggestions.'

Ethan smiled wryly. 'I'll bring those, too. And, Mia…before you go…' He crossed to the kitchen bench, picked up a largish envelope and handed it to her. 'They're a little hard to come by.'

'Er…thank you.' What were hard to come by? Puzzled, she slipped her finger beneath the flap.

'Don't open it *now,*' he said, thoroughly alarmed.

Mia stared at him.

'And don't open it on the way home either. Wait 'til you get there.'

'Er…right.' He seemed a little jumpy. 'Well, I'll be

getting along, then. Me and my sealed envelope full of hard-to-come-by things.'

Ethan's smile charmed her. 'You'd rather stay for breakfast?'

'No.' Definitely not. Because then she'd start wondering what it would be like to tease him over breakfast after spending the night making love to him all over his wickedly comfortable lounge chairs and plush pile floor rug. 'I'll see you Friday.'

Mia made it back to the hotel, back to her suite, before giving in to temptation and opening the envelope. Another quote, she'd figured on the way home. One that required a seat, a fan, and a glass of iced water handy while viewing it. But it wasn't a quote.

Photos.

About a dozen of them in total. All of them depicting a delicate beauty of a woman with flyaway black hair, almond-shaped eyes, and a face Mia recognised from the mirror.

There was one with Lily in a strapless black gown and elbow-length gloves, her eyes alight with laughter as she turned towards whoever had taken the photo. Two others showed a translucently beautiful Lily and a young Ethan playing on the beach. Happy times.

The rest were of Lily alone, and the sadness in her beautiful brown eyes wrenched at Mia's heart. With a trembling hand she spread them out on the table and drank in the details of the face staring back at her.

Her eyes filled with tears, so she went to the sideboard and poured herself a glass of water.

When the tears had gone, and she could see again, she came back to them.

She went to the sunroom when her eyes welled up again, and waited.

When she could see the skyscrapers of Butterworth on the other side of the channel she went back to them.

She went to the bathroom mirror and stared searchingly into it.

And thought of them.

Later—much later—she picked up the phone and dialled Ethan's number. 'It's Mia,' she said, when he answered. 'I—' She couldn't explain what it meant not to have to imagine what her mother looked like. Not to forever wonder which parts of her own face were her mother's and which were hers alone. Finally, *finally,* her mother had become real. 'I opened the envelope.'

'Are you all right?' he muttered.

'Thank you, Ethan,' she said softly. And hung up.

CHAPTER FIVE

Less than a week later, work on the hotel began in earnest.

'I wish you'd come and stay at the Hamilton while this is being done,' said Ethan, but Mia shook her head.

She didn't want to stay at the Hamilton. She liked being in the middle of it all. They were standing in the hotel foyer, watching the lowering of the chandelier. Moving it had been out of the question, so they'd opted to lower it and build a room-sized plasterboard box around it for protection while the rest of the work got under way. It had seemed like a good idea at the time. Mia figured it would work.

Ethan had said it would work.

'I like it here,' she said mildly, amidst the din of hammering and the whine of electric drills.

'Uh-huh.'

Mia smiled as the chandelier inched lower, the two men working the winch in the roof engaged in loud and rapid conversation with the three men on ladders guiding it down. 'Will they mind if I take a few photos?'

Ethan called out to them, and one of the men grinned and yelled something back which set all four of them to laughing. 'The one in the middle wants you to make sure you get his good side. The others are offering suggestions on what that might be. You probably don't want to know the exact translation.'

Mia got the shot, and with it the laughter and the ribbing. 'Tell them I'll put the photos up on a board outside the office if they want to come and take a look.'

'Team-building already, Mia?'

'Who? Me?' He looked so reluctantly amused that she snapped a shot of him. 'I'm just taking photos. Meanwhile, once baby's in her box—' she took another shot of the chandelier '—I'm off to Little India to look at fabrics for the furnishings.'

'You're not going to get an interior designer in?'

'Probably. But they'll work with what I give them. Look at this place, Ethan. Squint a little. I'm thinking bold, vibrant colours and contrasting textures. Velvets, silks, suedes, heavily embossed cottons...'

'I'm almost afraid to ask what colour you plan to paint the walls.'

'A cool white with a hint of palest green. I've seen it in one of the basement rooms.'

'The old colours,' he said with satisfaction.

'What are *you* doing after this?' she asked him. 'You could come with me.'

'Oh, no,' he said. 'Not me. There'd have to be thousands of bolts of material in some of those shops, and you'll have to look at all of them. And then there's the shopkeepers themselves. They *know* you're going to be there all day. They bring out tea, order in lunch, and by the end of it all there's *nothing* they don't know about you.'

'So that's a no?' she said. 'And you're probably going

to tell me not to mention that I'm scouting fabrics for this place.'

'Not a word,' he said firmly. 'They'll never let you leave. And don't go to Madame Sari's. She'll make the connection between you and Lily in a heartbeat, and from then on it'll only be a matter of seconds before she discovers why you're in her shop. And don't go to the one two doors up from her either. They'll recognise you there, too.'

'What's *that* one called?'

'I can't remember.'

'What if I go into it first? By accident?'

'Don't dwell on it,' he said. 'And don't order the chapatti.'

'I'll be strong,' she said. 'Ruthless.'

Ethan groaned. 'It's like contemplating the slaughter of the innocents.'

'I think you *want* to come fabric-scouting with me,' she said sagely. 'Women can tell these things.'

'No! No, I don't,' he countered emphatically. 'I just don't know if my conscience will let you go alone.'

Mia rolled her eyes. 'Honestly, Ethan. I'm not going to place an order at this stage. Especially not a big one. I'm just looking.'

'That's what they all say,' he said morosely. 'And then they see it. The one. And reason leaves the building.'

'Well, I'm leaving *this* building from round the side entrance in fifteen minutes,' she said with a grin, as the chandelier inched to a halt just before the bottom-most crystals touched the drop cloth they'd spread on the floor.

Ethan sighed heavily. 'I'll be waiting for you in ten.'

* * *

Fabric-shopping with Mia was everything Ethan had dreaded and more. Little India bustled and pulsed, Mia lingered and sighed, and he stoically endured.

He thought they were done with shopping when the last of the fabric shops had been thoroughly explored. His thoughts turned to sanctuary, to an afternoon gin and tonic at the Gentlemen's Club, because he deserved it, but Mia wasn't done with shopping yet.

'What do they sell in here?' she wanted to know, coming to a standstill outside a narrow red-fronted shop with Chinese signage.

'Chops.'

'As in lamb chops?'

'As in inking stamps. Seals. Signatures. *Chops*.'

'I need one,' she said.

How could she possibly need one? Until two seconds ago she hadn't even known what they were. 'Of course you do,' he said with a sigh, and followed her into the chop shop.

The walls inside the shop were papered with samples of the various stamp patterns the proprietor had made. There were chops in Tamil, Malay, Mandarin and English. Chops listing a person's name in both English and Mandarin, one after the other. 'These ones are good for cheques,' he said, pointing them out. 'Just stamp and sign.'

Mia looked around in wonder. 'It's just like a tattoo parlour.'

'Er...right.' The notion that Mia might have a tattoo somewhere on that delectable body brought all thoughts of inking stamps to a halt. 'You...ah...have a tattoo?'

'Well, no.'

Ethan struggled with equal measures of relief and disappointment.

'But I do like tattoo *shops*.'

'Mia, you like *all* shops.' He felt he could speak with authority.

'I could get a chop made up for the hotel,' she said.

'It already has one. It's very old, very beautiful. Ayah will know where it is. You might want to take a look at it and see if you want to use any of the design elements in it before jumping in and ordering a new one.'

'You're probably right.' Her dismay was comical.

'Nothing to stop you from ordering a personal one, though.'

'We also supply combination names for the modern couple,' said the shopkeeper, eyeing them both. 'Very popular. Household of your name and his name, and below it the household address.'

'Er…no,' said Mia hurriedly. 'That really won't be necessary.'

'You have something against the household of Hamilton and Fletcher?' asked Ethan wickedly.

'You mean Fletcher and Hamilton, don't you?' she said. 'F coming before H in the alphabet.'

'Nope. I meant what I said.' Ethan grinned as Mia bristled indignantly. 'Good thing this is a theoretical conversation, otherwise we'd have to get two made.'

'I can do a special deal for two,' said the shopkeeper. 'Even better special package deal on four chops. Your name, his name, and both names—swap-swap. Covers *all* correspondence. Excellent choice. I can have them ready for you tomorrow.'

Mia glanced helplessly at Ethan. Ethan's smile widened. 'You were the one who wanted to come in here,' he muttered. 'You explain.'

She didn't even try. 'I'd like one chop,' she told the shopkeeper firmly. 'With one name on it. Mine.'

The shopkeeper passed her a pen and a sheet of paper. 'Name and address.'

Ethan watched as she wrote her name and then stopped. 'Problems?'

'Yeah. I don't know which address to put down. Sydney or here. Which one's home?'

He couldn't help her with that.

'May I suggest *two* chops?' said the shopkeeper. 'One for each address. More if you have more than two residences. Very useful.'

'You're absolutely right,' she said. 'I'll get one of each. I don't *have* to decide which place is home right now.'

'Good call,' muttered Ethan.

'I know. We'd have been here all day. Can you imagine how many other chops I'd have been talked into by then?'

'We should shop together more often,' she said as they left the shop. 'We haven't had an argument or talked family for three whole hours. We've been bonding.'

Was that what she called it? Probably best not to mention the time she'd draped that amber velvet across her body and stopped his breath completely. Or the time the sun had caught her eyes, turning them to silver and catapulting him into a memory that wasn't his. He was more than happy to try and forget those particular moments himself.

'Where to now?' he asked her.

'I do believe I'm done with shopping for the day. I'm thinking of taking a trishaw home.'

'Tourist.'

'Chicken.'

'I am *not* being hauled around behind a bike on a seat surrounded by coloured lights, demigod talismans and plastic flowers,' he said adamantly.

'Of course you're not,' she said soothingly.

They went home in a plain black one.

They arrived back at the hotel without mishap, and stepped into chaos.

'Power is off!' the foreman told them emphatically. 'Off! Two weeks!' And then he launched into a loud and adamant discussion with Ethan.

'They're finding live wires everywhere,' Ethan translated for her. 'He wants to strip the lot and rewire completely before he reconnects to the mains. He's bringing in a generator. They'll run their tools off that. I've told him to tell all the men to pay particular attention to safety.'

Mia nodded.

'Which brings us back to what I was saying earlier. You now have no power, no hot water, and plaster dust everywhere. You really should consider staying elsewhere—at least for these next couple of weeks.'

'Do you think you could find a room for me over at the Hamilton?'

'Mia—' He eyed her in exasperation. 'There are two hundred and twelve of them.'

Ethan left her to her packing after that, telling her to call and he'd send round a driver for her whenever she was ready. It wasn't as if they'd be living in one another's pockets, she told herself for the hundredth time. There was a world of difference between staying at a man's hotel and living in his house. She'd probably hardly ever see him. He'd be up there in his penthouse, and she'd be in a regular room on one of the floors. He'd use the penthouse lifts; she'd use the regular ones. He'd eat in his quarters; she'd eat out. Why, they probably wouldn't see any more of each other than they already did, and that was working out just fine.

Except for when she'd put her hand in his as he helped her into the raggedy trishaw and heat had swept through her like a forest fire. Or when he'd settled beside her and stretched his arm along the back of the seat, recklessly turning the entire ride home into an exquisite form of torture.

He'd known exactly what sort of effect he was having on her. His eyes had flashed indigo, daring her to comment, but she hadn't said a word and neither had he.

Mia waited until the workmen had finished up for the day before hauling her bags down to the foyer. She left them at the door while she walked from room to room, savouring the quiet and the progress they'd made in a day. She made sure all the ground-floor windows and doors were locked up tight, because for the first time in years there'd be no one in the hotel tonight. No caretaker staff, no weary travellers. She made a mental note to ask Ethan if they needed night security staff, and with her tour completed set her suitcases outside and locked the door behind her.

Huge industrial bins of wall and ceiling plaster, the innards of the old hotel, stood waiting beneath the portico. Waiting to be hauled away. Cursing her sentimentality, Mia unzipped her shoulder bag, reached for her camera, and took a photo of them. She'd called a taxi on her way out rather than bother Ethan, but it hadn't arrived yet, so she wandered along the hotel front and took a few more photos while she waited. She took a shot of the lift the roofers had put in place, a shot of the scaffolding the painters had erected. The transformation had begun.

A man walking towards her on the footpath paused and stood with his hands in his pockets, surveying the hotel. An older man, with pepper-coloured hair, wearing casual trousers and a white shirt with the sleeves rolled up to his elbows. A tourist, she thought as he started towards her again, but then he looked up, looked at her, and stopped abruptly, his face draining of colour.

Not a tourist. Not even just a regular passer-by.

Nathaniel Hamilton.

She recognised him from Lily's photographs. This was the man her mother had fallen so deeply in love with.

This was Ethan's father.

He started walking again, walking slowly towards her, and she turned and walked back to her bags. Unless the taxi turned up in the next minute or so he'd have to pass by her. That or cross the road.

He didn't cross the road. He nodded when he drew level with her, his eyes intent on her face for the briefest moment, and then he averted his gaze and kept right on walking.

'Wait!'

He stopped, turned back, and the hope in his face turned her impulsive outburst into stupidity. She didn't want to give him hope. She didn't know what she wanted from this man, or what she was prepared to give.

'Do you walk past here often?' she asked haltingly.

'Every now and then,' he said, hope fading and weariness taking its place. 'It's good to see work begin here again. It's been too long.' He looked at her, looked at the suitcases. 'I would offer to carry your cases for you,' he said with the hint of a smile. 'If I knew where you were going.'

To your hotel, she thought confusedly. To take advantage of your hospitality, and that of your son. 'I— ah—there's a taxi coming.'

'Ah.' He went to walk on.

'I'm taking a room at the Hamilton Hotel,' she said in a rush. 'The one here in Georgetown. Temporarily.' She thought he might introduce himself then—she'd given him the perfect opening. But he didn't.

'I hope you enjoy your stay,' he said, after a moment's hesitation.

'Yes,' she said awkwardly. 'Yes, I dare say I will.'

He walked on, his movements slow and measured, and this time she didn't call him back.

'No,' said Mia firmly. 'Absolutely not.' She and Ethan were standing in the hallway on the top floor of the hotel, the door to his penthouse on one side of them, a door he'd just unlocked with an electronic gadget attached to a key ring on the other. 'I don't *want* the penthouse opposite yours. I want a room. A regular, everyday room.'

'You might want to cook,' he said. 'Spread out. You could be here a while.'

'I'll make do. Preferably several floors down.'

'You're afraid of heights?'

'No.' Just of living so close to him. 'I can't afford it.'

Ethan eyed her exasperatedly. 'You can afford it, Mia, but that's hardly the point. You're not paying for it. We put guests in here complimentary all the time.'

'Fine,' she said. 'Put me somewhere else.'

Two minutes later they were two floors down, and Ethan was showing her a regular luxury suite as opposed to a penthouse one. It had two bedrooms, a good-sized living and dining area, and a spa in the bathroom. 'This is as regular and everyday as you're going to get from me, Mia, and it is still a complimentary suite. Take it or leave it.'

'I'd rather pay for it.'

'Comp me at the Cornwallis sometime,' he said with a crooked smile. 'I like to check out the competition every now and then.'

'Done.' She felt marginally better about accepting his hospitality now that she had a way to repay it. But she still didn't feel quite right about it, and she knew why. 'I met your father a little earlier,' she said somewhat awkwardly. 'At least I think it was him.'

'Where?' Ethan eyed her sharply.

'Walking by the Cornwallis Hotel. He didn't introduce himself.' Mia shrugged and applied herself to the onerous task of deciphering the remote control on the table. She pressed a button and the curtains in the living area slid open. 'Neither did I.'

'Why not?'

'It was easier not to.'

Ethan sent her a level stare.

'May I ask you a question, Ethan? A family question?'

'I thought we agreed not to talk about family.'

'We did. And you haven't. And as far as preventing arguments between us are concerned it's working a treat. But I wanted to tell you I'd spoken to your father, and seeing as I've just broken the no-family-talk rule I figure I may as well sneak a few personal questions in on the side.'

'What do you want to know?'

'Why Lily never remarried. She stayed with your father for twenty-four years, raised you, loved the both of you. Why didn't she marry him, Ethan? Didn't he ask her? Didn't he want to marry again?'

'He asked.' Ethan smiled wryly. 'Repeatedly. And Lily refused him.'

'They didn't try to have more children?'

'I don't know. I don't know if it was a decision they made, or if it simply never happened, but there were no more children. I don't have all the answers for you, Mia. I doubt my father does.'

'He's here, isn't he? He's the one covering for you while you help me?' Helping her, indirectly, to realise her dream for the old hotel.

'He's putting in a few hours here and there. I suspect curiosity about work starting on the hotel got the better of him. I doubt he expected to see you. He does know your feelings about him, Mia.'

Mia sighed. 'I'm still not ready to meet with him. Not properly. When I've sorted out my feelings for Lily... When I understand what she did and why... When I've forgiven her, forgiven them all—*then* I'll meet him. With an open heart, Ethan. It's the only way.'

'I'm not arguing with you,' he said. 'I agree with you, and wish you strength. Ghosts of the past are hard to conquer, harder still to forgive. I gave up years ago.'

She opened her mouth to ask him about his ghosts, and Ethan put his finger to her lips, the brief scrape of his finger halting all thoughts of anything but him. 'We're done talking about this,' he said gruffly.

No, she thought, they weren't. But she kept her silence anyway.

Ethan sought solace in his penthouse after that, staring out to sea as he contemplated Mia's thoughts on forgiveness. He was no stranger to ghosts of the past—no stranger to rage mingled with regret, guilt mixed with defiance. He'd never been able to forgive Arianne her infidelity. Never forgiven her for dying the way she had. Beautiful, irresponsible, *selfish* Ari; she'd been all those things and more. Smart, funny, cunning. And his. She'd been that, too. Once.

Had he loved her? Had he *ever* loved her? He didn't know.

Damn sure she'd never loved him.

He couldn't forgive her. Wouldn't. He wasn't like Mia, still searching for something that might help him make sense of it all.

He had his answers.

And he hated them.

CHAPTER SIX

ONE week passed, and then another, and the days slid into routine. Work on the hotel ran smoothly ahead of schedule, and Ethan worked hard to keep it that way. He worked harder still to keep his dealings with Mia businesslike and, more importantly, brief. And still his respect and admiration for her grew. She'd thrown herself into the project wholeheartedly, and had staunch allies in Rajah, Ayah, and the rest of the hotel crew.

She'd taken to helping sort and clean the hotel furnishings and fittings with enthusiasm—so much enthusiasm that they'd relocated the site office from the library to the basement, where the sorting took place. Any labourer bold enough to get past Rajah and Ayah was likely to leave with an iron, a kettle, or a toaster in dubious working condition, and an invitation to stop by with their wife, mother, or auntie one lunchtime and pick through the linen in the next room. Mia's generosity had been rewarded with lunchtime curries, samosas, and an avalanche of invitations to christenings, weddings and various local temples.

She'd been absent from the sorting room these last two afternoons, though, and noticeably preoccupied when she *was* there. She'd told Rajah she was fine, but that hadn't stopped the old man from fussing over her. It hadn't stopped Ethan, and everyone else, from wondering what was wrong either. Theories on Mia's preoccupation ranged from homesickness, to delayed grief at her mother's death, to *someone*—and here more than a few glares had been directed at *him*—not taking the time to show her around the city and make her feel more welcome.

He'd left a message at Reception when he'd come in this afternoon, inviting her up to the penthouse. Business. Nothing more. Friendly concern for a colleague.

Yeah, right.

She arrived at his door at ten past seven, looking effortlessly elegant in slim-fitting fawn trousers and a casual sleeveless linen top. Emphatically *not* what she wore to work at the Cornwallis. More like something a woman wore when she wanted to impress a new acquaintance. Or a new lover. The thought snaked through his mind—a bright and ugly throwback to life with Arianne. He had no proof that Mia took casual lovers, and no reason to criticise her if she did. But his lips tightened at the thought of someone else's hands on her and his insides grew cold.

Grimly he ushered her inside. His need to know what she'd been doing and who she'd been with clawed at him, but he refused to let it hold sway. He just wanted to know what was bothering her. Friendly concern for a colleague.

Right.

'Rajah was asking after you this afternoon,' he said. 'He's worried about you. *I'm* worried about you.'

'I was here in your business centre on a conference call to Australia,' she told him, with the ghost of a smile.

Not a lover, then. Ethan ran a hand through his hair as he gathered up those other memories, slammed the door on them and rammed the deadbolt home. They had no place here. Arianne *would* not rule him from the grave.

'It ran a little longer than expected,' she continued. 'Nothing to worry about.' But she looked worried as she headed down the two steps and into the living area to stare out at the city below. 'Are these one-way blinds?'

'Yeah.'

'They're wonderful. Are you sure people can't see in?'

'Very.' The minute he said it he became uncomfortably aware that his living room at dusk was a little too secluded and the mood a whole lot too evocative for a business meeting. Asking her up here had been a bad idea all round. First Ari's hauntings, and now Mia herself, calling to him, always calling. The beast in him prowled back and forth, sensing weakness, but Ethan held tight to his control. 'I've had to take the tilers off the spa job and start them on the second-floor bar area.'

'Good,' she said. 'Fine.'

'No,' he said patiently. 'Not fine. Mia, you haven't heard a word I've said. And, seeing as you usually pay close attention whenever we talk hotel business, your preoccupation is a little unusual.'

'Sorry.' She turned to look at him, her smile wry. 'What were we talking about again?'

'The spa area.'

'Right. The...'

'Underwater lighting. They've sent the wrong fittings. So I've sent them back and started the tilers working on the second-floor bar area instead.'

'Good,' she said. 'Fine.'

He stared at her in exasperation. 'Are you going to tell me what's wrong?'

'No,' she said. 'I'm thinking not.'

'Does it have anything to do with the hotel?'

'Not exactly. Not with anything you're involved in, at any rate.'

Not exactly reassuring. 'What *does* it have to do with?'

Mia looked at him uncertainly, looked away again quickly. 'Money.'

Ethan waited for her to continue.

'My father's blocking the sale of some of my assets. If I can't sell them I won't have the money to complete the renovations.'

'It's not an insurmountable problem,' he said carefully.

'No, I can borrow against the hotel.' Mia tucked a strand of hair behind one ear and continued to stare out of the window. 'I just don't know if it'll be enough.'

'You could open the project up to investors.'

Mia nodded. But she didn't want to, he could tell. 'I'll try the banks first.'

'Why don't you try me first?'

'I—' She looked back at him, startled.

'How much do you estimate you'll need?'

'You know the cost estimates, Ethan. You put them together. Right now I can cover just over half.' Which left a shortfall of some ten million dollars. 'I can't borrow money from you, Ethan. I won't.'

'Why not?'

'Because it wouldn't be right,' she said stubbornly.

'The money's there, Mia. It was there for Lily, but she wouldn't use it either. What *is* it with you Fletcher women and this hotel? What is it that makes you so damned hard to help?'

'Ethan, you help plenty. You're practically managing the project as it is. Don't you think you do enough?'

'Are you complaining about the way I run things?'

'Why the hell would I do that?' she snapped. 'You're saving me a small fortune in management fees alone. More, if you factor in how good you are at it. I've never seen your equal, Ethan. Not even my father.'

'Is that supposed to be a compliment?'

'It *is* a compliment,' she said, shooting him a dark glare. 'My father's a brilliant businessman.'

'But a lousy father.'

'Don't you criticise him! He's a good man. He's hurting, that's all.'

'Hurting you.' He could see it in her eyes.

'He can't help it. He doesn't want to.'

'He doesn't *have* to.'

She looked away, turned away, and Ethan sighed heavily. He was out of line, criticising her father. But not that far out. 'All right, fine. You don't want money from me. What the hell *do* you want?'

She looked back at him. Just looked at him.

'Not that,' he said hurriedly. 'That is a *very* bad idea for us. We agreed on that last time.'

'We agreed we weren't going to talk about family either.' She took a step towards him, and it was all he could do not to step back. 'Are you scared of me, Ethan?'

'Only a little.' Only a *lot*.

'It's not going away, is it?' she said solemnly. 'Whatever this is between us. It's just getting stronger.'

'No,' he said, doggedly. 'No, it *is* going away. I haven't thought about you like that in...oh...' *Seconds.*

Mia's lips twitched.

'Ages,' he said firmly. 'In ages. Maybe this wasn't such a good idea,' he muttered. 'Inviting you up here.'

'Finally something we agree on.' She stepped closer. He didn't step back. 'I just want to see,' she muttered, almost to herself. 'I don't understand. Maybe if I understood more I could fight it.'

'Good plan.' Her lips tilted as she stepped closer, raising her hand to his chest, covering his heart. His body responded instantly. Ferociously. 'Bad plan.' But Mia didn't seem to be listening. Her gaze seemed to be fixed on his mouth. 'Mia—'

Too late. Her lips whispered across his, warm and tantalisingly lush, inescapably familiar. He fought it—the rush of sensation, the overwhelming need—clenching his hands to stop himself from reaching for her. Her hand slid up across his shoulders to curve around his neck as she drew away a little, her eyes searching his face. And then she tilted her head and kissed him again, another one of those fleeting meeting of mouths—only this time her tongue came out to delicately trace the curve of his lower lip.

And that was the end of his resistance.

He opened his mouth and her tongue met his, teasing, exploring, but not for long. Her lips became more urgent, more demanding, and he met her demands, passion, for outrageous, uncontrollable passion as her scent filled the air and his hands sought the warmth of her flesh. Learning the feel of her, knowing it already, he dragged her closer and gave hunger its due.

One touch, one kiss, fierce and urgent, and Mia was his.

Every gasp, every shudder of her wayward body was for him.

He knew exactly where to touch her, how to arouse her, but the advantage wasn't entirely one-way, because somehow she knew the same of him. Her thumbs rubbing across his nipples through the thin cotton of his shirt would make him tremble. An open-mouthed kiss to the base of his throat would make him groan. Like that. Exactly like that. Every urgent caress, every sound, every taste, inexplicably engraved in her memory.

She didn't care that he had the power to make her heart bleed; she'd become a creature of the moment. Nothing else mattered but Ethan. Her fingers found the buttons of his shirt, seeking skin and finding it. Another groan escaped his lips and she fed on it, fed on him, as he picked her up and carried her to the sofa.

They sank down onto it as one, her knees on either side of his thighs as he snaked his hands in her hair and his lips met hers for yet another one of those soul-stealing kisses. She could feel his erection pressing into her, hard against her softness. She wanted his mouth on her breasts and he knew it, dammit, but he made her wait while he nibbled on the curve of her jaw and pressed kisses along her throat.

He could take her now, just like this, and she wouldn't give a damn. On the sofa, on the floor, from behind. And if he did that... The thought of him making love to her exactly like that whipped through her and she arched beneath the lash of it. 'Ethan, please—'

'What do you want?' he muttered roughly.

'You. It's always you. In me.'

'You shouldn't.'

But his hands moved beneath her camisole, pushing it upwards, and his knuckles brushed the lace of her bra on the way back down. Back and forth, back and forth, over her nipples, until she screamed with wanting.

Her abandon was Ethan's undoing.

With savage intensity he took what she dared to offer, pushing her bra roughly aside and closing his mouth over her nipple, suckling hard, using his teeth on her and his tongue. He wanted her screaming. Pleading. Begging. Wanted her beneath him, lost to everything but the feel of him inside her. He could do that to her. He knew he could.

Knew damn well he shouldn't.

For a million different reasons, and all of them valid.

With a harsh groan he took his mouth from her, setting her bra to rights with shaking fingers before easing back against the chair and closing his eyes to the sight of her, another groan escaping him as his erection pressed between her thighs. If he couldn't see, he wouldn't take. Theoretically. His chest heaved as if he'd just run for his life. His heart threatened to escape his chest as he struggled for control.

'Mia—' He had no idea what to say. 'We shouldn't.'

'Dammit, Ethan! Don't you think I *know* that?'

He opened his eyes just a fraction. She was so beautiful. So dangerous.

'Get off. *Now.* Please.'

With a muttered oath Mia pushed away from him, scrambling from his lap and fumbling with her shirt as she put some much needed distance between them. She walked to the window, tucking a stray strand of hair behind her ear with trembling fingers as she stared down at the Padang below. She'd only meant to kiss him... just kiss him, that was all. How the hell had she unravelled so fast?

'What's happening to us, Ethan?' she muttered, when the silence became intolerable.

'You think *I* know?' he muttered. 'Maybe it's just lust.'

'Or a classic case of wanting what we can't have. I do that a lot.' She'd wanted a mother for the best part of her life. Not that it had done her any good. She turned back towards him, watching as he stood up, ran a hand through his hair, and started to pace. She'd wanted to know what he looked like with his shirt half undone and his hair all tousled, she remembered wryly.

Well, now she knew.

'Or we could go with lust,' she conceded. 'It's a goodie, and it's definitely up there as far as options are concerned. But what about the memories?'

Ethan's dark gaze clashed with hers. 'I really don't want to talk about the memories.'

Mia ignored him. 'Half the time I don't even *see* you in this day and age, Ethan. I see you with a sword in your hand and your hair tied back in a warrior's braid, or in monk's robes with hardly any hair at all. Everything's different except for you. How do you explain that?'

'I think we're going to have to switch religions to explain that one.'

She slid him a sideways glance.

'Or...we could ignore it,' he said. 'Denial being very good for the soul.'

'Something you learned during your monk phase, no doubt?'

'Probably.' A tiny smile tilted his lips. 'I expect I learned the value of retreat in the face of total annihilation during my sword-fighting phase.'

'I wish *I'd* had a sword-fighting phase,' she said glumly. 'I could have learned it as well.'

'Concentrate on the present,' he said firmly.

'Not sure that's wise. The present is a lust-filled disaster,' she reminded him. 'I'm short of cash, all but estranged from my father, totally confused about the maternal instincts of my recently deceased long-lost mother—and what do I do? I lust after you.'

'Women do that a lot,' he said sagely.

'Lust after you?' She could understand that.

'Multi-task,' he corrected. 'If you were male you'd be able to concentrate on one problem at a time and ignore the rest.'

It actually sounded like a halfway decent plan. She could do male. She'd been raised by one, trained to think like one, surrounded by them all her life. How hard could it be? 'So which one should I start with? The impending cash crisis?'

'Definitely,' he said. 'Your cash flow problem is your number one priority.'

'What's next? Lusting after you?'

'No. Then your relationship with your parents, living and dead, which will conceivably impact on your willingness to meet my father.'

'*Then* lusting after you?'

'No. Getting the hotel up and running will take up all your time after that.'

'When do I get to tackle the lusting after you problem?'

'Nowhere in the foreseeable future.'

'It's a good plan,' she told him, politely enough. Fatally flawed, of course, because right now, in his dimly lit apartment at dusk, the only thing she *could* concentrate on was him.

Which meant, she decided, with some semblance of rational and possibly masculine thought, that it was time to leave. She looked down at her camisole and tried to smooth the wrinkles from it. That was the trouble with linen—crush it and it stayed crushed. 'How do I look?'

'Dishevelled,' he said, looking up at her. 'Why?'

'Because I'm about to leave, and I'd rather not get into the lift looking dishevelled.'

'If you'd taken the rooms opposite you wouldn't have *had* to get in the lift,' he reminded her darkly.

'Yes, well. Moving on.' She smoothed her hair back over her shoulders and wiped her lips with the back of her hand, just in case any lipstick remained—not that it was likely. 'Now how do I look?'

'Wanton.'

Wanton was good. Wanton was several classes above dishevelled.

Wanton was deliberate.

'It's Friday night,' she told him. 'You should be relaxing. Kicking back, undoing a couple more of those buttons. I, on the other hand, should be sorting out my current cash crisis. So I'll be going. Which means that you—' she slanted him a smile '—can concentrate on whatever problem *you* intend to concentrate on tonight.'

Ethan glared at her. No prizes for guessing that the intensity of their lovemaking and his distinct lack of physical release could quite conceivably end up at the top of *his* list.

'By the way, I love this room at dusk,' she murmured. 'It makes me want to just lie back on your sofa and watch the lights take over the city below. And your floor rug here, so thick and soft. I could lie on that, too. And close my eyes and picture a lover's hands on me, and his mouth. Yep,' she said looking around. 'This room at night-time could quite possibly make a woman want a man more than she wants to breathe.'

'You're tormenting me deliberately.'

His eyes glittered with a warning she chose to ignore. What did he expect? Thinking like a man was all well and good when it came to business, but when it came to salvaging some small sliver of pride Mia far preferred to think like a woman. 'Blame it on my courtesan phase,' she said over her shoulder as she headed for the door. 'I'm pretty sure I had one.'

CHAPTER SEVEN

ETHAN cursed her after she left. Stalking from one end of the room to the other as he willed his body to settle. From the moment Mia had introduced herself and he'd looked into eyes of purest grey he'd known she had the power to captivate him. He didn't like it. He'd have given anything not to want her the way he did.

But there didn't seem to be a damn thing he could do about it.

She got to him. Whether shopping for chops or talking over ideas for the hotel or determinedly trying to make sense of her parents' actions she got to him—in ways he couldn't explain. He dreamed of her. Oh, how he dreamed of her…pliant and yielding beneath his touch. She had the power to make a man surrender, to make a man weep. He'd wept for her before. In his dreams…

She could steal a man's soul but she wouldn't have his. No, she couldn't have his.

There would be no more touching Mia Fletcher, and emphatically no more kissing her. He had to stop thinking about her, stop reaching for her in his dreams. He had to.

Because if he didn't, eventually he'd take what he craved. And if he did that...

If he did that, they'd both burn.

Mia's smugness over leaving Ethan wanting didn't last long. She'd taken his advice and started working on her cash flow problem once she got back to her room. The problem was the figures didn't look good. She could put the hotel up as security on the loan, possibly put her Brisbane penthouses up as security as well, but even with that kind of guarantee in place she still wasn't confident that a bank would loan her the money.

The Cornwallis Hotel lost money, and had for a very long time. A complete refurbishment was no guarantee that it wouldn't *continue* to lose money once it reopened. Her track record with regards to investments and portfolio-building was good, but she had no track record whatsoever when it came to renovating and running a hotel.

For four more hours she ran the figures and considered her options, juggling her portfolio elements until she found the most attractive option possible.

And still the figures didn't look good.

On the upside, she *had* just spent the past four hours not thinking about Ethan and what they'd just done. And not done...

It was a win. Of sorts.

The following Monday she contacted her banker in Australia. By midday she had her answer. No. The bank would rather do business with Fletcher Corp than with her. Fine. She tried another Australian bank, and then another. The reasons varied, but the answer stayed the same.

No.

On Wednesday morning she met with the investment manager of one of the big Penang banks. He didn't say no. Nor did he say yes. They'd prefer a guarantor, he told her, ever so politely. Or at the very least for her to have a substantial source of income that was independent of the hotel. They simply weren't prepared to take the chance.

She called her father.

'Mia,' he said guardedly, when he finally answered the phone.

'I'm opening the Cornwallis project up to investors,' she told him steadily. 'I just wanted you to know.'

Silence.

'If you want to invest in it, the offer's there. I'm letting forty-five per cent go, and you have first offer. I can have the prospectus to you within the hour.'

'You're wasting your money, Mia,' he said gruffly. 'You'll never get it back. Chances are you won't even turn a profit. The running costs on the place are exorbitant. They always have been. That won't change.'

'If the hotel caters to an exclusive enough clientele it won't have to change,' she said evenly. 'I know the money end of things needs to make sense to you. The figures aren't great at first, admittedly. There's a lot of initial outlay.' She ran a hand around the back of her neck and started to pace from one end of her hotel room to the other. 'Probably too much. But the long-term profit looks quite respectable. The investment is sound. Not great. But sound.'

'Give it up, Mia. Come home.'

'Daddy—' Her hands shook, her entire body shook, but her resolve stayed firm. 'I'm not sure I want to come home. At least not on a permanent basis. I miss you. I miss you very much. But I don't miss the business. For the first time in my life there's something else I want more. I love it here…this city and its people. I love this old hotel. And I think that when the renovations are finished—when the hotel is open for guests—I'll stay on and manage it a while. You're welcome any time. You're my father, you'll always be welcome. But I can't give this place up the way you did. I won't.'

She took a deep breath. 'So I'm looking for help. You were right. Even if I do sell everything I own I can't cover the cost of all the work that needs doing. The banks won't touch me. I need investors. You have first option. If I don't hear from you by the end of the day I'll assume you're not interested.'

'You're making a mistake,' he said. 'All I'm trying to do is protect you.'

'Don't.' With a quiet click, Mia hung up.

Ethan found Mia sitting at a table for two in the Hamilton Hotel's à la carte restaurant, a pitcher of water on the table beside a loaded fruit platter. He hadn't seen much of her these past few days. He didn't know if it was a deliberate move on her part or an unavoidable one on account of her chasing around for more money. But it was time he found out.

She looked drawn, melancholy, and utterly, utterly desirable, but she offered up a smile when she saw him and he pretended not to notice that it was decidedly lukewarm. 'Mind if I join you?'

'I'm snacking before dinner.' She waved him towards the seat opposite. 'Help yourself.'

He took a seat, eyeballed the fruit. 'How goes the cash flow problem?'

'Well…' she said slowly. 'I'm working through my options. The banks weren't altogether enthusiastic about lending me any of their money, and my preferred investor declined the opportunity, but that's okay—he's a little short-sighted. I've no doubt others will find the investment opportunity quite appealing.'

Ethan's heart went out to her. 'You asked your father, didn't you?'

She nodded.

'And he refused?'

She nodded again, looked away.

'I *told* you not to multi-task. Dammit, Mia! Why set yourself up to be kicked back down?'

'Because I love him,' she said quietly. 'Don't start with me, Ethan. I'm not a victim. I know what I'm doing.'

He fumed in silence, poured water into the glass in front of him, poured more into hers. A distraction, nothing more, while he worked the angles.

'So you need investors?' he said finally.

'I'm letting go of forty-five per cent. That should be enough to see the renovations through and cover the hotel's running costs for the first twelve months.' She picked up her water and sipped. 'I'm sending the prospectus out to investment houses in Australia and Penang tomorrow.'

'That won't be necessary.' There was nothing else for it. 'You already have an investor. Me.'

'No,' she said emphatically.

'You don't think we'd work well together?' He sat back in his chair, prepared to fight her all the way on this. 'We already do.'

'It's not that.'

'You don't think we share a similar vision for the hotel?' He knew damn well they did. When it came to plans for the hotel they were of distinctly one mind. 'You know we do.'

'That's not it either.'

'I can assure you I'm financially sound, if that's what's bothering you,' he said dryly.

A smile touched her lips. 'It's not.'

Which left the small matter of his wanting to devour her every time she came close. 'And it's not as if we're going to be mixing business with sex. Take the other night in the lounge room, for example. There was an... attraction there, granted, but did we follow through? No. We made a rational decision not to pursue a sexual relationship.'

'Speak for yourself,' she muttered. 'Every time we touch I *never* want to stop.'

Ethan sat back, shifting uncomfortably as certain parts of his body sat up and started paying close attention to the conversation. Great. Just what he needed.

'It's a good solution, Mia. A practical solution.'

'No, Ethan, it's not. Working with you until a decent project manager becomes available is a practical solution. Convenient. Surprisingly easy. *Temporary.*' Her cool grey gaze seared him. 'There's nothing temporary about going into business with you. And nothing fleeting about my desire for you. Disturbingly timeless is the phrase that comes to mind.'

Ethan stared at her, thinking through her objection.

She had a point. She did have a point. But her more im-
mediate problem was a financial one. 'What if I could
prove to you that we could manage our attraction for
one another? That we can make it go away?'

'How?'

Yes—how? The finer details escaped him. 'We'll go
on a date,' he said at last.

This time her smile did reach her eyes. 'Yeah, I can
see how that'd help.'

'Hear me out. We go on a date now—tonight. And I
will bet you the chance to buy that forty-five per cent
stake in the Cornwallis that nothing happens between
us.'

'Define *nothing happens between us,*' she said cau-
tiously.

'Casual touching is allowed,' he said, thinking fast.
'For example, I might put my hand on the small of your
back as I escort you through a door. I'd do that with any
woman.'

'Fair enough,' she said. 'Very chivalrous of you.
What about kissing?'

'Kissing is allowed in moderation,' he said. 'A kiss
on the cheek at the end of an evening often means nothing.'

'I'll keep that in mind,' she said. 'What about lovemaking?'

'Lovemaking is *out,*' he said firmly. 'If we wind up
in bed together, you win.'

'I certainly do,' she murmured.

Ethan eyed her sternly. 'It won't happen, Mia.'

'You're that sure?'

'Yes.'

'I do like confidence in a man,' she said, with a decidedly feminine smile. 'I'm in. So where do we start?'

'Right here—with dinner.'

'Here? As in right here?' Mia sighed heavily. 'I guess you were thinking of a casual date as opposed to a wildly romantic one.'

'You don't think this is romantic?'

'Well, the candles are a nice touch, and I do like the red décor,' she said, looking around. 'But it's not exactly a winner as far as romantic environments go, now, is it? There are people everywhere, for starters. And look how you're dressed—a business suit! Look how I'm dressed!' She stared down at her trousers, flicked at the cuffs of her white-collared shirt. 'The girl equivalent.'

'See?' he said. 'You're annoyed with me already. I told you this would work. We eat right here. I'll even make sure it's charged to your room,' he said, working hard to make this a date she'd remember with a shudder.

'You're *paying* for my room, Ethan. And every other service the hotel provides—something you neglected to mention, but the woman in the business centre was kind enough to point out when I tried to pay for my time there.'

'Didn't I mention it? I suppose I could always withdraw those particular services,' he said with a grin. 'But, seeing as how you look exceedingly annoyed about them, I may as well let them stand.'

'Idiot.'

He was on a roll. 'By the way, I agree with you completely about your clothes. They just won't do.' He paused for effect, contemplated a dried fig, picked it up and took a bite—nope, not that one—and put it back on the platter. 'You could always try wearing a dress.' He'd never—come to think of it—seen her in one. 'That's if you have one.'

'Oh, I think I could hunt up a little something.' Her smile came slowly. 'Maybe I could even find some high-heeled shoes to go with it. Do you like high-heeled shoes, Ethan?'

'Whatever.' Ethan shrugged as nonchalantly as he could manage with the vision of Mia in stilettos and very little else running amok in his brain. 'Where would you like to go afterwards? Sports bar? Trishaw races? Cockfight?'

'Dancing,' she said, with the quirk of an elegant eyebrow.

Ethan smiled back. 'I know this really good transvestite escort establishment not far from here. Five, ten kilometres away maximum. We could walk there. Great dance floor. You'll love it.'

'Oh, I don't think we need to venture quite that far.' Her smile was positively evil. 'It just so happens I have a ballroom.'

Dinner was the easy part. Dinner consisted of a Thai-style seafood platter for two, a side of rice, and green salad. Waiting the fifteen minutes it took for Mia to get changed into something a little more appropriate was excruciating, but Ethan survived by heading up to his suite for a shave and a change of clothes of his own. Not clothes inspired to turn her off, just a white shirt and trousers. His attempts to turn the date into a disaster had proven fruitless. Mia was better than him at games. He knew that now. From now on he was playing this date straight down the line.

Denial all the way.

He made it back to the foyer with a couple of minutes to spare, and organised for one of the hotel limos to pick them up. The sooner they got there, the sooner they could leave. And then Mia stepped out of the lift and all rational thought ceased.

She wore a strapless red dress that clung tightly to her body and stopped well short of her knees. It had been designer cut to make a man drool, he'd stake his life on it, but he held firm and kept his jaw off the floor. Until he saw her shoes. Strappy little red sandals, they added at least four inches to her height, and a sway to her hips guaranteed to drive him insane. Her hair shone black and glossy, her lips were coloured a deeper shade than usual, and her eyes shone silver with laughter and no small measure of challenge.

'I see you've changed into something a little more comfortable, too,' she said when she reached him. 'No tie.' She smoothed the collar of his white dress shirt flat, as if it wasn't already perfectly pressed, and smiled a siren's smile. 'Not that you'll be needing one.'

'Right.' Ethan swallowed hard. He could handle this. The dress, the shoes, Mia... The limo pulled into the drive and the doorman signalled him discreetly. 'Our ride's here.'

'Does it have fairy lights and plastic flowers?' she purred.

'Just leather.' Lots and lots of leather. Damn near the same colour as her eyes. 'The champagne is optional.'

'Oh.' She sighed with a disappointment he knew full well was faked, and her dress sighed right along with her. 'Never mind, that sounds quite pleasant, too.'

She sashayed towards the door, much to the delight

of the waiting doorman and chauffeur. It'd take a stronger man than he was to keep his gaze from sliding to her rear end. Not that there were any in the room.

'I'll drive,' he told the chauffeur, who stood waiting by the car with the rear passenger door open. 'Tell Reception you're down to one hotel limo for the night.'

'Yes, *sir*.' The chauffeur grinned, shut the rear door, opened the front passenger one, and wordlessly handed Ethan the keys. Mia eased into the car with effortless elegance, first her delectable behind, and then her legs and those cherry-red shoes.

Necks craned. Ethan glared.

Mine.

Not exactly the most auspicious start to a platonic evening of... Ethan muttered a silent prayer...dancing.

'We just need to make a little stop somewhere along the way,' she said when he'd settled into the driver's seat.

'What for?' he asked warily.

She smiled artlessly. 'Music to dance to.'

They stopped at an electronics stall on the outskirts of Chinatown where Mia bought a twenty-ringgit CD player—complete with batteries. The next stall provided them with the CDs to go in it. When she asked for Viennese waltz music Ethan heaved a sigh of relief. He could waltz. Kind of. Had she picked up music to tango to he'd have been in trouble in more ways than one. All that touching.

All that skin.

She picked up two other discs in rapid succession and handed them to the storekeeper. More waltz music. Had to be.

They moved on to the Cornwallis after that, the hotel looming secretive and silent in the darkness. 'Are you sure you wouldn't rather go somewhere else?' he said hopefully. 'Somewhere with light and…oh, I don't know…people? People would be good.' There were over a million people on the island. Surely they could find *some* of them.

'This'll be better.'

Sighing, Ethan slid the key into the kitchen service door and held it open for her. She had the CD player in one hand, the discs in another, and she slid past him with a smile he found distinctly unsettling.

'I meant to ask you if we needed permanent night security for the hotel,' she said, looking around the darkened, partially built commercial kitchen. 'We're probably getting to the stage where we need it.'

'I'll sort it,' he said.

'There was one other thing…'

'See?' he said encouragingly. 'You're not thinking of seducing me at all. You're thinking business. What does that tell you?'

'That I can multi-task?'

'I've warned you about that.'

'I don't know what Ayah and Rajah's living situation is,' she continued blithely, 'but I'm wondering about offering them the caretaker's rooms as part of their new wage package,' she continued.

'You want them to do more?'

'I want them to do less,' she said. 'I want them to take on some sort of upper management supervisory-and-training role which, as they get older and the hotel runs smoother, will get less. A semi-retirement plan, you could call it, with accommodation supplied and a full wage attached.' She sounded defensive. As if she expected him to argue against it. 'Sixty years is a long time, Ethan.'

He knew it. And was inordinately glad Mia had thought to their future. 'They live with one of their sons and his family. Living space is tight, but it's never been a problem. You could offer the caretaker's rooms. It may suit them. I don't know. But they're proud people, Mia. Emphasise the importance of the work they'll be doing, and the benefits of having them on site. They won't accept charity.'

'Got it.'

'Another investor could quite conceivably be unhappy about that kind of generosity,' he pointed out mildly. 'I, on the other hand, wouldn't have a problem with it.'

'Shut up, Ethan.'

'Or that,' he said, slanting her a warning glance. 'Much.' They'd reached the ballroom. He opened one of the doors and waited for her to step inside. The chandelier in there had been lowered and boxed up, too, and the smaller sidelights taken to the basement for cleaning. 'I'll get some torches from downstairs.'

'Do you really think we'll need them?' she said, with the lift of an eyebrow. 'There's moonlight coming in through the windows. I can see just fine. Moonlight is very romantic, don't you think? As is music.'

She put the CD player on the floor, slipped a disc into it, pressed the play button, and turned up the sound. The sultry notes of a lone saxophone filled his ears and Mia filled his eyes as she sauntered past him, looking over her shoulder as she lifted her hands above her head in an age-old gesture of abandon and began to move in time to the music. He'd never seen anything more erotic.

'What would you like to talk about?' he asked, a touch desperately.

'Do you always talk while you're dancing, Ethan?'

He wasn't dancing. 'How do you feel about the melting polar icecaps?'

'Despondent,' she said, and moved closer, not touching him—not yet. 'Possibly in need of comfort.'

'Yes, well. Perhaps we could look into making the hotel as energy efficient as possible?'

'Mmm. You're not dancing, Ethan.'

'I'm thinking about it.'

'Maybe if you take your hands out of your pockets?' Hers were still above her head, her wrists exposed, and her eyes were half closed as she met the music passion for passion.

'Maybe this isn't such a good idea,' he said huskily.

'Really?' Her gaze met his, sultry and knowing. 'Where's all that stern resolve?'

Gone. 'Dancing's not exactly my forte.'

Her smile turned wicked. 'I'm sensing some reluctance here, Ethan.'

So much for using conversation as a distraction. There was nothing for it but to move closer and set about explaining the rules. 'Here's how it works,' he said. 'Casual touching is allowed while dancing.'

'How about meaningless cheek-kissing?'

'How about we save that for later?'

Mia smiled. 'You really think this is going to work, don't you?'

'Yes,' he said, with far more confidence than the situation warranted. 'And tomorrow morning you'll have no more cash flow problems and a brand-new business partner.'

The curve of her lips mesmerised him. The sway of her body, so perfectly attuned to his own, seduced him. He brought her closer, whisper-close, until her body brushed his with every slow, sensual move she made. He slid his hands down her body, finding curves, exploring them. 'We can do this.'

'There's just one problem,' she said. 'You see, I'm exposing a great deal of skin here. Whereas you—' she slid her hand between the buttons of his shirt and almost set him on fire '—are all buttoned up. I can hardly test my resolve if you're all buttoned up, now, can I?'

'Yes,' he said, and cleared his throat. 'Yes, you can. You can test your resolve to *keep* me all buttoned up.'

Too late. The top button of his shirt slid free of its hole under the onslaught of knowing fingers; the rest of them came loose in rapid progression. 'There,' she said in satisfaction as she smoothed his shirt aside. 'Skin. Equality has been restored.'

Pity about his equilibrium. Because that had just disappeared.

She stepped in close and slid her arms around his neck. *His* hands went to her waist as her body melded with his, every achingly familiar inch of it. 'Yes, that ought to do it,' she murmured. 'I'm feeling *very* tempted now. How about you?'

'Not at all.' He whirled her around and set her against the wall, releasing her abruptly and planting his hands on either side of her, palms flat against the wall, for good measure. Now he wasn't touching her at all, and still the spell she wove whispered in the air around him. 'I can resist you,' he muttered.

Her hands dropped to her sides and she stood there motionless, watching him, just watching him, with those wary grey eyes. She lifted her face and her lips moved towards his, stopping millimetres away, not touching him—not quite.

He didn't move. Couldn't.

She sighed, a tremulous little sigh, and her lips brushed his, whisper-soft and ever so fleeting. They stood there like that, not kissing—not quite—for what seemed an eternity.

And then the music stopped.

He stepped away, turned his back on her, and battled for control. Air—he needed air. He went to the doors that opened out onto the elephant landing in order to get it. He would let the sea in, and his memories of Arianne's deceit. Surely that would help him resist Mia? The doors creaked open and the breeze darted in, mischievous and unpredictable, whipping at Mia's hair as she came up beside him, whipping at her dress.

'I'll *give* you the money to finish the renovations,' he said as he turned towards her, shoving his hands in his pockets so they wouldn't reach for her.

'No.'

No. Ethan smiled mirthlessly and kissed his sanity goodbye. 'What other kind of music do you have?'

'Shostakovich.'

Passionate and Russian. Not a lot of help there. 'Make it a waltz.' Waltzes had structure. One hand on her waist, the other holding her hand. None of that up-close-and-personal stuff.

'I can do that.' She walked back towards the CD player and he watched her—heaven help him, he watched her all the way. Watched her kneel to change the music, then stand and turn as gracefully as any dancer and walk back towards him. She stopped a good ten metres before she reached him, flicked her hair behind her shoulders—and waited.

'You're going to be very, very good at this, too, aren't you?' he muttered.

'I've had a few dance lessons here and there.'

Ethan sighed. He really should have guessed. The evidence had been overwhelming. The way she walked and sat, the graceful way her hands moved when she was describing what she wanted to the builders...

The music came on. Clarinet and strings. Elusive, like the wind at his back, as he walked towards her. He stopped a foot away from her, took her hand in his and set his other hand to her waist. He could do this. He could. And then she stepped closer and slid her hand beneath his shirt, and he breathed her in and shuddered hard.

'Casual touching's allowed,' she whispered. 'You said so yourself.' Her hand slid to his shoulder, to the proper waltz position. He'd have been just fine with that. He would. If her hand hadn't been *beneath* his shirt.

'When the music stops, so do we,' he muttered huskily.

'What if the music doesn't stop?' she said as they began to move. 'What if it's a ten-minute waltz? Ten minutes is a long time, Ethan. Who knows what could happen?'

'Nothing,' he said as he drew her closer—not that he meant to. 'Nothing is going to happen. It's just a dance.'

'You're wrong.' Her hand slid from his shoulder to his nipple, sending a tremor straight through him. They were hardly moving, Mia's hands were on his chest now, and his went on her waist, drawing her closer, always closer. He had to taste her—just a little taste. He'd pull back after that. He would. He bent his head, seeking her lips and finding them, soft, so soft, and then she closed her eyes and the music soared and spun him into madness.

He nipped at her mouth, impatient for her to open for him and overwhelmed when she did. He knew her taste, drank it down, desperate for more, always more. He knew the feel of her, needed to feel all of her.

And the music stopped.

Pulling away from her was almost impossible, but he did it, putting space between them, an ocean of space, as he walked over to the CD player and pressed the stop button. 'I'll *loan* you the money,' he said huskily. 'Bank rates and terms.' Anything to make this insanity stop.

'No.'

Ethan scowled. 'What other music do you have?'

'Drums,' she said.

Drums were good. Surely drums wouldn't encourage kisses?

'Japanese drums.' She fed the disc into the machine and stood to face him as rhythm, pure and bold, echoed through the room and called to his soul. He *knew* this music in the same haunting way he knew Mia.

'I have these memories of you,' she said as she moved into his arms. 'Of us. And sometimes it's slow and dreamy...' Her hands slid across his chest, sending a tremor straight through him. 'And sometimes not. You really shouldn't have let the wind in. Or the sea. Because we can do fast and elemental, Ethan. We can do it very well.'

And then her lips were on his, and the last of Ethan's

resistance shattered into glittering shards at his feet. He let the wildness come, and with it his need for her. He could take her now, right here on the floor or against the wall, and she'd let him. Peel her out of that temptation of a dress, slide into her and drive them both insane. He knew he could.

So much skin, so creamy and soft. He couldn't get enough of it, enough of her. She broke the kiss to fumble with his belt buckle, and he cursed and pushed her hands aside before threading his hands through her hair and crushing his lips down on hers for a kiss that left him shaking with the need to possess her.

Right here, he thought incoherently as he edged them towards the shadows. Right now, as they slammed up against the wall, Mia pliant and willing as she clung to him.

He couldn't stop. Not this time.

Mia whimpered as Ethan's tongue met hers and duelled. She slid her palms across his nipples and his fingers tightened in her hair. His kisses grew deeper, but it wasn't enough. She squirmed against him, aching for more, and he gave it to her, pulling away only long enough to tug at the bodice of her dress with a rough, unsteady hand, and then his tongue flickered across her nipple, hot and wet, before he drew her into his mouth and suckled hard. 'Ethan, please...'

His chest heaved as his arm curved around her bottom to lift her up, bracing her against the wall as she wrapped her legs around him. He was fully aroused, overwhelmingly male, and—dear God—she prayed he wasn't about to stop. His fingers traced the line of her panties and immediately she wanted them off—couldn't see how to get them off without leaving his arms, and that was impossible.

'Rip them,' she muttered, and almost flew apart in his arms when he did as she commanded. He slid his fingers between her legs, teasing the tiny nub there, but it wasn't enough. Not nearly enough. 'Ethan, please...'

'Please what?' he muttered roughly.

'Please *me.*'

'Some courtesan you are,' he said, sucking in a breath as she fumbled with his belt buckle, clumsy in her haste to touch him the way he was touching her.

'Some monk you are,' she whispered when she found him.

Ethan cursed and pushed her hand aside before he exploded—for it wouldn't take long. He surged against her, skin to soft and heated skin, not in her, not yet...

He parted her with his fingers, savouring the slickness and the heat, before setting himself in place and slowly demanding entry.

Mia gasped as he penetrated her, her body stiffening, resisting him—dammit!

'What is it?' he muttered, intent on his task.

'Big,' she muttered back.

'Relax.' His grin was slow and confident as he slowly pulled back, easing her discomfort, positioning her for maximum drag on a certain part of her anatomy as his mouth captured hers, soothing and reassuring. *Damn,* but she loved his initiative. He slid back inside her, and this time her body accepted more of him. Slow and easy, deeper, further, as the pleasure built and her body grew accustomed to him. She appreciated his restraint, she really did...but it wasn't enough. Not with this man.

She slid her mouth free of his kiss, set her lips to his

ear and whispered two short, succinct words that she'd
definitely learned during her courtesan phase. Seeking
the wildness in him.

Finding it.

Ethan felt his control snap at Mia's whispered words.
He surged into her, hard and fast, and she took him all,
again and again, her hands clawing at his shoulders and
her breath coming in gasps as she tightened around him,
arching, shuddering.

Screaming.

He felt her go over, felt the ripples start deep inside
her, consuming her, consuming him. Passion drove him
now, and he bucked beneath the lash of it, a harsh groan
rumbling up from his chest as he emptied himself deep
inside her. Rearing, pulsing.

Surrendering.

Ethan shook in the aftermath, his chest heaving and
his breathing laboured as he tried to come to terms
with what he'd just experienced. Not sex. Not lovemaking. He knew both, and this was different again.
Unstoppable, ungovernable.

Inevitable.

He pulled back, composure eluding him. What could
he say? He'd failed dismally in his attempt to prove they
could resist each other. He'd fail again before the night
was through.

'Are you all right?' he muttered gruffly. 'Mia?'

She didn't look at him as she set her clothing in order,
her breathing as ragged as his, her body not quite finished its trembling.

'You did ask for it.'

'Yes.' She shot him a wry, half-rueful glance through eyes still cloudy with passion. 'I know.'

He saw to his own clothing with shaking fingers. 'Ask for it again.'

CHAPTER EIGHT

MIA woke on the plush pile carpet of Ethan's window-lined living room with Ethan sprawled beside her, deep in sleep. They'd made it back to his apartment but hadn't quite made it to his bed before their craving for each other had taken them again—a powerful unstoppable force that neither had been able to control.

Her need for him had been insatiable, and he'd matched it—oh, how he'd matched it. In this, at least, they were equals.

Whether his need for her would still be there this morning was anyone's guess. She had to be ready for him to step back. Mia closed her eyes, took a deep breath.

She wasn't anywhere *near* ready for that.

Maybe with distance…

Time…

She got to her feet slowly, so as not to wake him. Found her shoes beneath the coffee table and her dress behind the sofa. She scooped them up and took them with her as she padded silently from the lounge area, hesitating when she reached the end of the open-plan area and had the choice of turning left, right, or putting her clothes on where she stood and heading for the door. She needed a bathroom. Had no idea where to find one.

'Third door to your left,' said a voice from behind her, and she whirled around to find Ethan standing there, buck naked, watching her through wary eyes. 'You want me to go down to your room and find you a change of clothes?'

'I…ah…' She looked down at the dress in her hand. Thought about the lift ride and the long walk to her room two floors down. Someone was almost bound to see her. A hotel guest. One of Ethan's employees.

'It's not a trick question, Mia. I just thought you might prefer to leave here wearing fresh clothes,' he said, running a hand through his hair as he turned away from her and scooped up his trousers.

The operative word being *leave*.

'Yes,' she said, dismayed by the wobble in her voice. 'Of course. Just get…whatever. I…ah…might use your shower while you're gone.'

'Third door to your left,' he said again, and disappeared through a doorway to his right.

He'd directed her to the guest bathroom, Mia decided when she found it. For there were no men's toiletries to be found. Just a basket of feminine fripperies and a surfeit of plush white towels—the kind that turned up in her hotel bathroom every morning.

She dropped her shoes and her dress on the floor and stepped into the shower, swatting away the memories of Ethan's lovemaking as fast as they arrived. She was out of her depth with this man. Wanting things she knew instinctively that he wouldn't be able to give. Marriage, children, love… She wanted it all, but he'd offered nothing.

Not nothing, a tiny voice whispered from the deepest corners of her mind. They'd shared something last night. Something wild and beautiful.

Not nothing.

The bathroom door opened a few minutes later and Ethan came in, fully dressed, with her clothes under one arm. He set them on the bench, met her gaze in the mirror and she paused, breathless, as his eyes raked her body, hot and possessive. Slowly, deliberately, she lifted her hands to her hair and tilted her head back, her gaze never leaving his face.

Not nothing.

He stood motionless for what seemed like eternity, until finally, finally, his hands went to the buttons of his shirt. Relief washed over her, mingling with the water, mingling with the tears that pricked at her eyelids. Whatever they had, for as long as they had it, at least it was something.

'So we're not doing regret this morning?' she said huskily as he stepped into the shower, his body already blatantly, unmistakably ready for her.

'No.' He took the soap, turned her around and started to lather her back with it.

'What *are* we doing this morning?'

'Well, I don't know about you, but I'm taking what I want.'

'Ah,' she said, and very nearly whimpered as his lips grazed the back of her neck. 'Plunder.' Did he *know* how much she loved the feel of him at her back? She thought he did.

When his hands reached the curve of her hips and he drew her back against him, long, knowing fingers easing over her to cup her essence, she knew he did. She arched against him, bracing her hands against the wall and readying her senses for the slide of him inside her.

'What do *you* want?' he muttered.

'You. It's always you. Inside me.'

'It seems,' he said in a ragged, husky voice, 'that we have an accord.'

They made it to the breakfast table, made it through coffee and toast without awkwardness as they discussed the Cornwallis and the work slated for the day. They left awkwardness until she was ready to leave.

'This plunder plan,' she said hesitantly, 'is it an on-going plan?'

'Do you want it to be?' he asked, his expression guarded.

Mia shrugged and looked away, too afraid to tell him what she really wanted because she wanted it all. 'I know I want your hands on me.'

'When my hands are on you no one else's are,' he said in a tight, controlled voice.

'Dammit, Ethan. What do you think I am?' She turned back and glared at him, stepped in front of him, in his face, deliberately invading his space. 'Trust me— that one's a given.'

He nodded once, but whether he believed her or not was a different matter. Mia's eyes narrowed. 'I expect the same of you.'

This time his eyes flashed fire. 'You'll get it.'

'Good. All settled, then.'

'Not quite,' he muttered. 'I didn't think to ask you… mainly because I didn't think at all. Do you take birth control measures?'

'I do.'

'I just needed to know,' he said defensively.

'It's an important question. I don't mind you asking it. I would love a family, Ethan. I'd love to have children someday. But I doubt that's the kind of relationship you're offering.'

'It's not,' he said tightly.

'I have *no* desire to trap you, Ethan. *Absolutely* no desire to be a single parent. Just so you know.'

'If it turned out you were carrying my child, you wouldn't be!'

The temperature surrounding them had jumped a good ten degrees. The day was shaping up to be a scorcher. Or maybe it was just Ethan, spoiling for an argument? she thought with grim amusement. 'May I ask you a personal question?'

'No.'

'If circumstances were different…if you were married to a woman…deeply in love with her and you knew beyond doubt that she loved you…would you want children then?'

'Love fades,' he said harshly.

'Not always,' she said. 'Sometimes it can last a lifetime. Would you want children then?'

Ethan said nothing. Mia felt her heart falter. 'I'm thinking *double* safety precautions for us,' she said finally. 'Agreed?'

'Agreed,' he said gruffly.

'Is the aftermath of plunder usually as difficult as this?'

'Usually it involves walking away.' He eyed her darkly. 'Usually it's not hard at all.'

'Ah. Here I go, then. Walking away.' But not before

she'd stolen another kiss from him. One that rapidly threatened to spiral out of control.

'What are you going to do about the Cornwallis?' he muttered, when his lips finally left hers.

'Distribute the prospectus around to a dozen or so investment houses this morning. I've already contacted Bruce Tan. He'll handle the Penang side of things. I'll deal with the Australian investment houses myself. I have good contacts. I'll be in to work after lunch.'

Ethan nodded. 'I'll see you there.' And when her gaze went to his lips. 'Go. While you still can.'

'Miss Mia, we have an unforeseen but not entirely un-expected problem,' said Rajah later that day as they stood at a sorting table.

'Someone broke into the Cornwallis last night?' She'd heard all about it the minute she'd stepped through the door. The open ballroom doors, the abandoned CD player…

Thank God she'd picked up her underwear.

'Ethan's organising night security.'

'Most excellent, Miss Mia, although that isn't the problem I was referring to. This is a different problem.'

He'd get round to telling her eventually, Mia was sure of it.

'It's August,' he pronounced gravely.

'I see,' said Mia, and, after a moment's hesitation, 'No, sorry—I'm afraid I don't see. What happens in August?'

'The gates of hell roll open and the ghosts pour out,' said Rajah sagely.

'Ghosts,' she echoed.

'Hungry ones.'

'Here? In the hotel?' she said, and Rajah nodded. 'Ghosts?'

'Indeed so, Miss Mia. The men complain of misplaced tools turning up in the oddest of places, of lights dimming and doors slamming and a sneaky breeze that does not belong to the wind.'

'Oh.' *That* breeze. 'Right. So we need to…?' She eyed Rajah expectantly.

'Feed them, Miss Mia.'

'Of course.' And, after a moment, 'How?'

'By preparing a feast for them on the fifteenth day of the month. Until then it's best to keep them entertained. Plays. Operas. Dramatics.'

'You don't think daily restoration crises are enough? Couldn't they just tune in to those? They're *very* exciting.' For anyone whose money it *wasn't*.

'Clearly not, Miss Mia.'

'Pity.' Mia sighed. 'How do you know there's more than one?'

'Ayah will know,' said Rajah confidently.

Ayah did know. 'It's Yuen Chin—a Chinese courtesan spy, betrayed by her employer and beheaded by her lover,' she said decisively. 'She's been here for years. She used to seek revenge. Now she merely seeks peace.'

'Oh, good,' said Mia as her head thunked against the desk.

'You need to find out what's happening in room eighteen,' said Ayah.

'It's been gutted. New plumbing is going in today.'

'There's your problem. You've disturbed her.'

Oh, boy. Mia raised her head and tried to think like a long-dead murdered courtesan currently seeking peace. 'She'll settle,' she said at last, and, to Rajah, 'Tell the

men not to worry. Once that plumbing's in she'll be ec-
static. Women love good plumbing.'

Ayah nodded her agreement. 'She'll still be hungry,
though. No one gets fed in hell. You'll need food. Lots
of food. A feast.'

'You'll also need incense,' said Rajah. 'And light.
Incense *and* light in the form of giant joss sticks being
particularly helpful. Of course, being Indian, I'm unfamiliar with the finer details. You'll need a Chinese
scholar to advise you on those.'

Mia made a mental note to ask Ethan where she could
find one.

'Your mother researched her,' said Ayah. 'You'll find
Yuen Chin's history amongst her papers.' Ayah turned
and, after some thought, pointed to a group of boxes in
the corner. 'Perhaps over there?'

'How will knowing her history help?'

'You'll need to make offerings to her as well,' said
Ayah. 'One must know *what* to offer her.'

'Perhaps her conniving traitorous employer's head
on a platter?' said Mia, getting into the spirit of things.

'That'd be a start,' agreed Ayah.

'I'll tell the men you have the problem under control, then,' said Rajah, somewhat hurriedly. 'They *will*
be pleased.'

'Tell them about Yuen Chin,' said Mia. 'Tell them
we'll be entertaining and feeding her. And tell them
their tools should be returned to the storeroom every
afternoon and locked up for the night. Tell them that
particular order came from Ethan.'

Rajah smiled broadly. 'He's already given it,
Miss Mia.'

* * *

Mia hadn't planned on taking her mother's files on Yuen Chin home from work, but the story was impossible to resist. By the time Ethan turned up at her suite later that evening her bed was covered in ancient newspaper clippings she couldn't read, and meticulous notes written in a neat and feminine hand that she could.

'I didn't know Lily studied history,' she said, covering her pleasure at his seeking her out with whatever topic came to mind. She shut the door behind him and motioned him to sit where he would—which pretty much meant the edge of the bed. If he was careful.

'She had a weakness for stories,' he said with a crooked smile, opting to stand. 'I thought I might find you here. Yuen Chin?'

'Yeah. Lily thinks she was pregnant when she died. So sad.' Mia laid the sheaf of papers she had yet to sort through on the bed and gave him her full attention. She hadn't seen him at the Cornwallis earlier, for all that he'd said he'd be there. Probably a good thing, considering her tendency to want to relieve him of his clothes. 'I like your suit.'

'Thank you.'

'Pity about the tie.'

'You don't like it?' His lips twitched.

'No, it's as divine as the suit. I'm sure I could find a great many uses for it.' None of which required it to be around his neck. Her hands itched to touch him, but she kept them to herself. Surely this ferocious wanting would ease in time—wouldn't it? 'Rajah thinks we should celebrate the festival of the hungry ghosts and appease our murdered courtesan. He tells me it'll bring good fortune to the hotel and maybe even break the curse.'

'There's a curse?' said Ethan.

'How else would the hotel come to be in such disrepair?' Ethan opened his mouth and Mia held up her hand. 'Don't answer that. Anyway, feast night is fifteen days away, which gives us plenty of time to prepare.'

'Us?'

'Okay, me. Rajah thinks it should take place at the hotel. Somewhere outside in the grounds on account of all the fire, I think he said, although he's a little short on details.'

'You need to talk to Mr Kwong Senior when he comes in next. He'll know.'

'Ayah says we need to make paper gifts to appease her.'

Ethan nodded.

'Any idea what a courtesan would like as a gift?'

'Money,' he said. 'Money to burn. It doesn't necessarily have to be real. Best if it's not, given your current cash situation.'

'Yes, well, thanks for that,' she said dryly. 'I'll try and remember. Actually, I was thinking more along the lines of paper clothes and perfume bottles. Hair clips, jewellery, that sort of thing.'

'Weapons,' he said. 'A dagger.'

'A packet full of regular tea, a packet full of poisoned tea, and a tea set,' she countered. 'Daggers are overrated unless you plan to lodge one in someone's heart from a distance—and that's not nearly as easy as it sounds.'

'And you know this *how?*' he asked. 'I say keep the dagger and poison the tip, if you must. Daggers are useful.'

'Okay, the dagger stays. What about poisoned wine and a couple of goblets as well? I do like a woman to have choices. And when are you going to kiss me?'

'Not sure I'm game.'

'It'd be far worse not to.'

'Good point.' He leaned in without touching her, and set his lips to hers for a kiss that started out as a hello and quickly turned heated.

Waiting for him to arrive at work earlier in the afternoon had thrown up a few *more* questions about their relationship that needed clarifying, and she'd vowed she'd get around to asking them. And she would. Soon. Just as soon as she finished kissing him.

'I'm going up to shower and change clothes,' he murmured when he released her. 'You should come up.'

'Was that an invitation or an order?'

'What would you like it to be?' he said with a grin.

'If I told you I'd be the shame of the feminist movement. As it is, I think I'll stick it out down here for another hour or so, just to prove I can, and *then* come up. But you just go right ahead and take that shower.'

Ethan's grin widened. 'Come up,' he muttered against her lips, before standing and striding towards the door. 'Bring a change of clothes. You'll need them in the morning.'

'Masterful,' she purred. 'I'm all atremble. This being your pirate captain phase and my obedient one. I love this phase.' She glanced back down at the notes on Yuen Chin's life and grisly death, because if she didn't she'd never let him leave. 'It says here she had a sister who plotted to bring the wicked employer to justice. She was *still* plotting when she died of natural causes at eighty-eight. Yuen Chin should have a gift to take to her sister. What about a bouquet of flowers?'

Ethan shrugged on his way out through the door. 'Why not?'

* * *

'We need to talk,' said Mia some two hours later as she sat at Ethan's kitchen counter eating leftover Nasi Goreng from a takeaway food box. Ethan had eaten earlier, after his shower. Mia hadn't eaten at all, but she'd refused to order Room Service and have it sent up so he'd raided the fridge for something to feed her. Unfortunately neither the food nor the glass of wine he'd set in front of her seemed to have taken the edge off her restlessness.

'What would you like to talk *about?*' he asked warily.

'Guidelines.'

He was going to need a little more than that to work from. 'As in…?'

'Codes of conduct for our current relationship.'

'Couldn't we just talk about the weather?' Mia glared at him. No. Right. He cast about for something that could be worrying her apart from mindless sex overlain with memories that weren't theirs—or maybe they were—and the promise of absolutely no promises. 'Well,' he said finally, 'we sleep together.'

'When?'

'Whenever is mutually convenient,' he said carefully, hoping like hell that was the right answer. He'd never negotiated the shots before. He usually called them.

'How democratic,' she murmured. 'Where?'

'Wherever we want. Within reason.'

'Of course.' Mia smiled, and Ethan heaved a sigh of relief. Guidelines successfully negotiated.

'Last question,' she said, with a wave of her chopsticks. 'Do you want anyone to know about us?'

'You mean family?' he said. 'You're thinking of your father.'

'I mean anyone,' she countered. 'Rajah and Ayah,

the contractors, the hotel staff, the samosa vendor and, yes, my father. He'd probably disown me. On the other hand, he already has, so maybe that's not such a problem after all.' Her accompanying smile served only to strengthen the shadows in her eyes.

'It's a problem, Mia. You know it is.'

'Yes, well. I'm trying not to dwell on it. What would *your* father say?'

Ethan tried to think about it from his father's point of view. 'He'd probably want to know my intentions,' he said at last. 'Which could prove a difficult question. He wouldn't understand the plunder plan.'

'So…we're looking at a *clandestine* plunder plan?'

'I think so,' he said with a nod. 'Yes.'

'I've never had a relationship in a vacuum before,' she said mildly. She didn't seem altogether impressed by the notion, never mind that it neatly solved the problem of having to mention their sleeping arrangements to her father.

'The trick is to not think of it as a relationship,' he said firmly. 'Think of it as a visit to the gym.'

'Not sure the gym should be doing Nasi Goreng,' she said, looking down dubiously at the fried rice before setting it aside and turning a disturbingly penetrating gaze on *him*. 'So, what other benefits can be found in this…gym?'

'A bed,' he said. 'You'll like it.'

'I'm thinking massage,' she said archly. 'Unparalleled dedication to my body.'

'You'll get it.'

'Excellent.' Her gaze turned sultry. 'When?'

'Now. That is, if you've stopped thinking things through?'

Apparently she had. 'A bed, you say?' She sauntered around the counter towards him and touched her lips to his. Lightly, teasingly. Staggeringly potent. His hand came up to cup the back of her head as he slanted his lips across hers and dragged her into the maelstrom.

Her shirt came off before they were out of the kitchen. His tie came off halfway down the hall. 'There's a bed around here somewhere,' he muttered as she wrapped her legs around him and he slammed her into the wall. 'I'm sure of it.' He found the door handle around the time she found his belt buckle. Lost his breath about the time he lost his trousers.

When he finally tumbled her onto the bed he lost his mind.

He took her again through the night, and again, and each time she gave him whatever he demanded, and each time he lost that little bit more of himself.

He lay there in the darkness while she slept beside him and he tried to pretend it didn't matter. That he'd find all the little pieces of himself in the morning and they'd fit back together just the way they'd used to.

Even when she'd gone.

CHAPTER NINE

ETHAN found his father sitting alone in his garden, on a bench overlooking a twisted willow. Goldfish swam in the pond beside it and dragonflies flitted in the air above. He'd caught frogs here as a boy, scoured the edge of the pond for giant snails and co-operative lizards. Avoided the centipedes, kept a weather eye out for snakes.

'She used to come here every day,' said Nathaniel, by way of greeting. 'She knew every twist in that tree, every curve and bend, every new shoot. See that branch over there?' He pointed to a low branch overhanging the water. 'That's her life branch. She said it mirrored her life exactly. See how it changes direction at the gnarl halfway along? That was when she met us. And the smaller branch running off just before it, so slim and strong and young? That's Mia's branch.'

Ethan said nothing. He never knew what to say when his father spoke of Lily and Mia.

'Did you get to the investment houses?' asked his father after a moment.

Ethan nodded. 'The EN Corporation now owns thirty per cent of the Cornwallis Hotel. I transferred the money through yesterday. I couldn't get the last fifteen, though. They went to an Australian investment broker to distribute. By the time I found out which one they were gone. Bought by a shelf company very similar in set-up to ours five minutes after the prospectus landed on the broker's desk.' He paused. 'I have a theory.'

'I share your theory,' said Nathaniel with a weary smile. 'You think Richard has them.'

Ethan looked out at the twisted willow, at Mia's branch. 'I doubt it'll be a problem. Richard refused the full forty-five per cent and used a company I'm betting Mia doesn't even know about to pick up what he could afterwards. He doesn't want her to know he has them. *We* don't want her to know *we* have them. Between us we'll be the most amenable silent partners in history.'

His father regarded him curiously. 'I still don't see why she refused your initial offer to buy in. You're working well together. You said so yourself. Apart from that you're family, and you love that old hotel. I'd have thought she'd have *welcomed* you on board.'

'It's…complicated.'

'I'll try and keep up,' his father said dryly.

Ethan sighed. Nathaniel had just watched him take over six million dollars of company money and scoop up brokered shares—with all the associated costs— rather than buy them from Mia outright. He deserved some sort of explanation. 'Mia wants to be able to walk away,' he said gruffly. 'From me. She didn't think she could do that if we were in business together.'

'What do *you* want?' asked Nathan gently.

'To be able to let her.'

A tiny smile creased his father's face. 'She's touched you, hasn't she?'

'I really don't want to talk about it,' he said, desperate to change the subject. 'Which branch is mine?'

'That one.' His father's deep chuckle rippled out across the pond—a sound Ethan hadn't heard since Lily's death. 'That one right there, rubbing against Mia's.'

Work on the Cornwallis Hotel continued ahead of schedule. Ethan had never seen such a hard-working crew. A lot of their enthusiasm came from the way the old building responded to their ministrations, as if suddenly reaching sunlight after years of living in darkness. The rest of their enthusiasm came from the sense of involvement and teamwork Mia generated. She might not have any experience in the hotel business, or with restoration work in general, but the effortlessness of her people-management skills would make a Fortune 100 company CEO weep with envy.

Irritations turned into amusements, differences of opinions became collaborations—with spectacular results. She'd tacked Yuen Chin's newspaper clippings up on the picture board, along with an invitation to a feast in her honour, and turned a problem into an eagerly anticipated party and a project deadline to boot. Spirits had been consulted, auspicious dates calculated, and the night sky observed. The decision was unanimous. Work on the hotel would finish on the fourteenth day of the seventh lunar month.

And heaven help any worker who missed their deadline.

'So what do you think?' Mia had dragged him away from a mountain of paperwork to look at the spa centre, completed that morning.

Ethan looked, and found no fault with it. The workmanship was superb, the tiling subcontractor and his men worth every cent of their exorbitant fee. Even the dozen-shades-of-white interior, including marble accents, had come up warmer and more welcoming than he'd expected.

'They're finished with the bathrooms, too,' she said, and minutes later they were examining one of those. They'd used the same white-on-white treatment in these rooms as well, but Mia had insisted on retaining the quirkiness of old. A Renaissance frame surrounding a mirror in one bathroom, a silver elephant's trunk faucet with ears for taps in another, and—Ethan shook his head in disbelief—a bronze sleeping dragon handbasin in another.

It worked. He wasn't quite sure why, but it did work.

The painters had finished the north wing completely and started on the south, the pale green walls giving airiness to the spaces, accenting the warmth of the woodwork and picking up the colours in the marble to perfection.

She'd chosen well, thought Ethan in satisfaction. Now all she needed to do was find a decorator to take on the interior. They'd interviewed half a dozen so far, but Mia had proven remarkably hard to please.

'You need to get an interior decorator in place.'

'I haven't found the right one yet.'

He sighed heavily. 'You're going to be a girl about this, aren't you?' he said, as they left the bathroom with the sleeping dragon in it and headed for the door.

'I am a girl, Ethan. And the answer's yes.'

'Ahem,' said Rajah from the doorway. He was wearing his polite face—the one he reserved for building inspectors and city officials. 'Miss Mia, Mr Ethan—there's someone here from Madam Sari's to measure the windows.'

Ethan glanced at Mia.

'Curtain fabric quote,' she said readily. 'I figured if an interior decorator doesn't turn up soon I may as well start without them.'

'Dangerous,' he murmured.

'Yet strangely appealing,' she countered with a grin.

'Sanjay Ghosh at your service,' said the portly, middle-aged man beside Rajah with an air of importance at odds with the task he'd come to do. 'If I may trouble you to show me the windows requiring measurement?'

'I'm thinking all of them,' she said, and the little man beamed. 'But you can start with the ones in here. Thanks, Rajah.'

Rajah disappeared. Ethan thought about joining him, but curiosity, and a hefty appreciation for *anyone* on Madame Sari's sales team, made him stay.

'I'm Madame Sari's second favourite son-in-law,' Sanjay Ghosh explained, as he measured and recorded window measurements with a deftness that belied his portly stature. 'And *why,* may one ask, would *anyone* want curtains on these windows when timber blinds would look superb, cut down on noise and heat *and* pick up the colours in the floor? A ruched gauze to filter the light, if you *must*—which we can of course supply at an extremely reasonable price—but a full fabric treatment?' Sanjay shuddered. '*I* don't think so.'

'Does Madame Sari sell blinds?' asked Mia.

'Sadly, no,' he said. 'One must acquire blinds elsewhere.'

'No friend you know who can do us a deal too good to be true?' asked Ethan.

'Alas, not yet. Ask me tomorrow. By then I will no doubt be hustling for food scraps on account of losing such a contract, and enjoying the dubious joys of being Madame Sari's *third* favourite son-in-law. Fortunately her fourth favourite son-in-law is a lying, cheating, odoursome son of a camel, and occupies *that* position permanently. I'm really most fond of him.'

'I'd be fond of him, too,' said Ethan.

'What do *you* think about blinds instead of curtains?' asked Mia.

Ethan shrugged. 'You'd need costings, of course.'

'I do approve of the bed,' said Sanjay, eyeing the antique wooden frame—one of the pieces Mia had deemed worth saving. The window seat in the sunroom also met with his approval, as did a superbly crafted wooden coffee table. The four matching lounge chairs met with decidedly less enthusiasm, which wasn't surprising given the condition they were in. The wooden framework had withstood the test of time. The lumpy chair stuffing and threadbare fabric hadn't.

'I have bedcover and linen fabrics and several astonishingly beautiful yet reasonably priced furnishing fabrics that are simply *perfect* for this room,' he announced.

'Excellent,' said Mia. 'You can cost those out as well as the gauze for the windows. What do you know about interior design, Sanjay?'

'Enough to fill an ocean. It is a passion that came upon me as a child.'

'Anything a little more *formal* in the way of qualifications?' asked Ethan.

'Ask me tomorrow,' said Sanjay.

'Here's the plan,' said Mia. 'You and I are going to talk our way around the hotel, and you're going to quote on the fabrics you think would be suitable throughout. Ethan—' and here she sent him a warning glance '—is going to leave us to it.'

Ethan sighed. 'You're so innocent. It's charming. Really.' He shot Sanjay a warning glare. 'You've got two hours to talk your way through the hotel. Two days to get your quote in. And it *will* come past me.'

'I'll keep that in mind,' said Sanjay.

Ethan turned towards Mia. 'Come find me when you're done. You can tell me the worst of it then.'

'That sounds a lot like *second*-favourite-project-manager talk to me,' she said airily.

Ethan's eyes narrowed.

'I sympathise, my friend,' said Sanjay.

'I surrender,' muttered Ethan. 'See me later,' he told her, and left.

'He won't be a problem,' said Sanjay confidently. 'He *wants* to accommodate you, I can tell. Besides, he has impeccable taste in suit fabric.'

'Doesn't he just?' said Mia, and set about making her vision for soft furnishings and fabrics come alive.

'He's *very* good,' said Mia some three hours later, as she perched on the edge of the desk in the small room off the foyer that Ethan had commandeered as his site office. 'He does some reupholstering on the side.'

'Uh-huh,' he said.

'He took a library chair and a footrest away to do as a sample. If he gets the contract he'll include the work in the total costings. If he doesn't, there's no charge at all.'

'If he snags the fabric contract *and* the reupholstering of all the furniture you want to keep he'll be Madame Sari's favourite son-in-law for years.'

'I know.' Mia grinned 'I can't wait to see that chair. Apparently my eyes will be so dazzled by its splendour I may need to wear sunglasses—which Sanjay can also supply at a *very* good price. Maybe I'll get you a pair, too. Then I wouldn't have to see that look you're giving me. The one that says you think I have no idea how to do business here.'

'Keep an open mind,' he warned. He didn't want to dampen her enthusiasm for Sanjay's ideas—whatever they were—he just wanted to inject a little caution into the process. 'Wait until you see the upholstery job he does and the price he quotes you.'

'I *knew* there was a reason I didn't want to talk to you about this,' she said with a sigh. 'You're practical.' Her grin faded and her expression grew serious. 'Okay, I'll wait. I do know how to do business here, Ethan. I've been watching you and learning. I know to bargain hard and examine everything. I know to be very, *very* specific about what I want. I didn't *expect* Madame Sari's window-measurer to be an interior decorator, Ethan, but I found myself agreeing with ninety per cent of what he said and thoroughly enjoying the remaining ten— which was, I concede, the most outlandish sales pitch imaginable. He felt right for this place.'

Uh-oh. Woman's intuition. She was bringing in the big guns. 'Wait and see,' he said, as he stood and walked to the door and closed it.

Mia eyed the closed door warily. Eyed him. 'You

wanted to talk to me privately?' They'd done their best to keep their relationship from becoming common knowledge. During work hours they worked. Worked well together, as usual.

Usually they made a point of keeping their doors open.

'It's about money, isn't it? The shares sold through almost immediately, Ethan—honest. The money's in the bank. It'll be cleared for use within days.'

'It's not the money.'

'You're worried I'll go mad and spend a fortune on soft furnishings? Because I won't.'

'It's not that either—although I realise this will require restraint on your part.'

'So what do you want to talk to me about?'

'I have a dinner engagement tonight. Across town.'

'Fine.' She held his gaze steadily. 'Keep it.'

No objection. No angling for an invitation. He should have been pleased.

He wasn't. 'I'll be back late,' he said curtly.

Mia shrugged and tucked her hair behind her shoulders.

Dammit, if *she* had a dinner date that didn't include him he'd want to know some details! Like who it was with, and where. And when the hell she was going to be home!

'You don't mind?'

'It doesn't matter if I mind or not,' she said, with a welcome flash of temper as she took her butt off his desk and turned to face him. 'We have an agreement not to make this relationship public. So here I am. Keeping that agreement with as much dignity as I can. What more do you want from me, Ethan? An admission that

I'll miss sitting at your kitchen bench having dinner with you? That I'll miss having my hands all over you?'

'Will you?'

'Yes,' she muttered grudgingly. 'Satisfied?'

He was now. 'I'll make it up to you,' he murmured.

'An excellent idea.' She eyed him coolly. 'When?'

'This weekend. Which reminds me…' Ethan hesitated, wishing he didn't have to raise this particular topic again. But he'd promised his father, and Ethan kept his promises. 'My father has a house on the other side of the island. I have a standing invitation to turn up there for lunch on Saturdays.'

Mia stiffened.

Ethan sighed. 'He'd still like to meet you, Mia. The invitation includes you.'

'Dammit, Ethan! First you don't want to be seen with me and now you do!'

Here was the reaction he'd wanted from her earlier, when he'd talked about going to dinner without her. But no. She had to wait until he mentioned his father. 'This invitation has *nothing* to do with our sleeping together and you know it! You're Lily's daughter. My father would like to meet you. I'm happy to take you… when you're ready. If you're not ready, say so.'

'I'm not ready.'

'In that case I'll see you in a couple of days,' he said tightly.

'Fine.' If words could bite, that one would have left a cannon-sized hole in him. 'I might be around.'

Ethan said nothing.

'All right—you're right. I'm overreacting,' she said, crossing her arms tightly around her waist as she walked to the window. 'Maybe I *am* ready to meet him. Maybe

I just don't want to do it at his home. Couldn't we do cakes and coffee somewhere else instead? Or drinks after work in the downstairs bar at the Hamilton? Somewhere public?'

Ethan thought about it. Thought about Mia needing neutral ground. Somewhere she could be in control of her own coming and going. It wasn't an unreasonable request. 'If I arranged something like that, would you come?'

'Maybe.' Mia ran her hand through her hair. 'Okay, yes. I'm not ungrateful, Ethan. I'm staying at your hotel free of charge, you're helping out here, and your father's picking up Lord knows how much of your regular work. If you arrange something like that, I'll come.'

'He doesn't want your gratitude, Mia. If that's all you have to bring to this meeting then you're right. You're not ready.'

'I'm scared, Ethan.' She turned to face him. 'Scared I'll be betraying my father if I meet yours and like him. Scared of just how badly I want my mother to have loved me, missed me, thought of me, dreamed of me…' Mia shook her head. 'The way I dreamed of her. How could she walk away from me, Ethan? How? I still don't understand.'

'I think,' he said carefully, 'that she did it for love of your father.'

'That would be the one she *left*?' she countered, heavy on the sarcasm.

'Hear me out, Mia.'

She held his gaze and waited.

'I think she knew he still loved her,' he said simply. 'That his world would shatter without her. So she made the ultimate sacrifice. She gave him you.' He saw her eyes begin to fill with tears but continued doggedly on. 'I think your father's pain was so terrible that he *had* to cut Lily out of his life in order to survive. And that meant he had to cut her off from you, too. It wasn't a lack of love that guided them, Mia. Maybe it was just a little too much. *There's* your starting point. That's how it was.'

Mia nodded jerkily.

'But Lily's death changed everything, and now you have a say in how it's going to be. Forget about what my father wants or what your father wants. What do *you* want? Do you want to build a relationship with my father and get to know what Lily was like through him? Do it. Do you want two old men who were once the best of friends to sit down together at your dinner table? They owe you, Mia. Damn well *make* them do it! Take what *you* want out of this.'

A faint smile crossed her lips. 'So you'd recommend plunder?'

'Exactly.'

'Pirate.'

He felt like one, behaved like one, as he reached for her and drew her into his arms. Emotion. The air swirled with it. Mia fairly pulsed with it as her hand slid around his neck and she brought his lips down to hers, drawing him into her effortlessly, deliberately, until there was nothing but Mia. 'There's more than a little bit of pirate in you, too, Mia.'

'I know.' Her eyes darkened with pleasure as he ran his hands over her, drawing her close, making no secret of his arousal.

'Come home with me,' he muttered. 'Now. To my place.' He had to have her, had to satisfy his soul-deep need to possess her, to take and take until the world around them disappeared. 'Please.'

'Sometimes I wonder if it's the memories talking,' she muttered. 'Sometimes I wonder what the hell I'm doing.'

'You're not alone.'

Without Mia, Ethan's formal dinner dragged on—and it took a concerted effort to stay with the conversation and pretend interest. Only when talk turned to the Cornwallis and its refurbishment did he engage.

'Such a grand old dame,' said his hostess, a titled English octogenarian herself. 'I remember the balls we used to attend there back when the hotel was in its prime. Oh, the rakes we met there. That glorious ballroom. The elephants… Tell me, Ethan dear, why didn't you bring your stepsister along tonight so we could meet her? You *know* you're always welcome to bring a guest.'

'Auntie, *you* know I never do,' he said gruffly. The 'auntie' tag was an honorific frequently used in Malaysia as a mark of respect from the younger generation to the older one, and had nothing to do with being related. Ethan had called Lady Eleanora Jordie Auntie for as long as he could remember. 'And she's not my stepsister. Technically.'

'Nonetheless, I hear you make quite a team.'

'Mia inherited her father's business acumen,' he said as blandly as he could, while he fought to keep the memory of Mia in his bed this afternoon out of his brain. Her sleepy, satisfied gaze, her laughter when he'd looked at the clock, cursed, and hurriedly started throwing on clothes. He'd asked her if she'd still be there when he got back and she'd laughed again and said no, she had better things to do than warm his bed when he wasn't in it, and that if he wanted to see her when he returned from wherever it was he was going he could damn well come and find her. He'd smiled at that. Smiled again at the memory of it.

'Ethan, dear, you seem a little distracted,' said his hostess.

'Not at all.' He made a determined effort to concentrate on the conversation at hand. 'Where were we?'

'Mia.'

Business Mia. 'She's not difficult to work with. Usually she thinks like a man. Until today, when we started in on the soft furnishings. Then she started thinking like a woman.'

'Well, that's as it should be,' said Lady Jordie with satisfaction. 'I *must* meet her, Ethan. Where's she staying? What's her phone number? I'll call and invite her over for coffee and dessert. You'll go and get her, won't you, dear boy?'

'Ah…you mean *now*?'

'Of course *now*. I can't believe you didn't bring her in the first place. It's a perfect opportunity for her to meet people. Poor girl, she'll think she's been spurned by polite society. What were you *thinking*?'

'Don't be ridiculous,' said Mia adamantly, and Ethan held the phone a little further away from his ear.

'So that's a no?'

'Of course it's a *no*, Ethan. No one turns up to a dinner party for coffee and dessert.'

Ethan sighed. 'They do at Lady Jordie's.'

'Let me speak to her, dear,' said the lady in ques-

tion. 'I can tell you're not having much luck. Go prac-
tise your charm on some other young lady.'

'I heard that,' said Mia. 'And if you do I'll cut out
your extremely talented tongue.'

Wordlessly, Ethan handed the phone over and stepped
back. Way, way back. And grinned.

Two minutes later the lady of the house handed him
his phone. 'Such a sweet girl,' she said happily. 'We're
having lunch together next week, and then she's offered to take me on a tour of the hotel to look at the
renovations. Such a pity she couldn't make it tonight.
I assured her we'd all love to meet her, but she seemed
quite firmly against the notion for some reason. Not that
she *gave* me a reason. She said it was hard to explain
and she wouldn't know where to start.' Lady Eleanora
Jordie surveyed him regally through a pair of shrewd
and lively brown eyes. 'She said to ask you.'

Sanjay Ghosh's interior decorating quote arrived at nine
a.m. Monday morning. All sixty-five extensively de-
scribed and precisely illustrated pages of it. Along with
the requested quotes on curtain and bedding fabrics
were suggestions—and prices—for furniture, blinds,
louvres, floor coverings, and artwork.

Three enormous boxes of fabric swatches, bundled
and labelled according to room and purpose, sent Mia
into raptures and Ethan to muttering about budgets. The
prices were on the back, along with estimates of how
much fabric would be required.

'He's a visionary,' she announced once she'd reached
the end of the third box. 'We have to bring him on
board.'

'He's a window-measurer,' countered Ethan. 'He has no track record.'

'He will when he's finished with this place.' Mia couldn't get over how perfectly he'd captured the feeling she wanted for the hotel. 'Look at this stuff, Ethan. Look at the detail! How on earth did he put all this together in two days and have it make perfect sense? It's old-world elegance with warmth, luxury, and a dash of the absurd thrown in for good measure.'

'There's more than a dash there,' he muttered.

'It's perfect.'

'It's risky.'

Okay, so maybe he was right. 'What if we do a trial area first? Turn him loose on the north wing apartment? I'll show him the pieces I want to keep, give him a budget and a time frame, and if it's a disaster I'll learn to live with it. If we like it, we get him to do the rest.'

'Define *we*,' he said dryly.

'You and me.'

'What happens if we don't agree?'

'Worry, worry, worry.' She picked up the topmost batch of fabric swatches and passed it to him. These are for the foyer. Is there anything there you don't like? And look at the runner he's chosen for the grand staircase.' She waved a leaflet beneath his nose. No need for him to look at the price tag on that particular piece. 'It's absolutely divine.'

'It's Axminster. When were you planning to mention the *cost?*'

'Never.'

Ethan's lips twitched. 'What about your plan to move back into the north wing? When were you going to mention *that?*'

'Soon,' she said. 'Now.'

'You're not comfortable at the Hamilton?'

Mia eyed him in exasperation. 'I'm extremely comfortable there, Ethan. You know I am. But I can hardly accept your hospitality for ever. The Hamilton is *your* home, not mine. *This* is my home. Or at least it will be. Do you think Sanjay could have the north wing apartment ready in a week?'

'I think he could have the Taj Mahal ready in a week.'

Ethan's boyish smile lit up his face and stole Mia's breath. He smiled more and more these days. She figured he enjoyed bringing the old hotel back to life just as much as she did, figured the clandestine plunder plan was working out just fine for the most part. They'd lasted the week at any rate.

Whether they'd last another was a different matter.

'How does six-thirty in the downstairs bar at the Hamilton tomorrow night sound?' she asked him casually.

Ethan's eyes narrowed. 'We're not talking interiors any more, are we?'

'No,' she admitted. 'I thought I might invite Nathaniel to join me for a drink. I'd like you to be there.'

'Are you sure about this?'

'No…' But she had a picture in her head—a picture Ethan had put there—and this was the first step towards it. 'But I'm thinking I'll do it anyway. I'm thinking an hour or so of casual conversation, easy on the past and concentrating heavily on the now. How does that sound?'

'Ambitious. Bring a prop.'

'I am,' she muttered. 'You.'

'Bring another prop,' he said. 'Bring Sanjay's quote. That'll entertain us all.'

'So...' She drew a deep breath. 'Do you want to invite him or shall I?'

'I think,' said Ethan with a gentle smile, 'that he'd much rather hear it from you.'

At precisely six twenty-five the following evening—armed with a thimbleful of bravado and clutching Sanjay's interior design quote as if she'd never let it go—Mia strode into the bar.

Ethan and his father were already there, sitting in two comfortable chairs by a window. A third chair sat empty, and a small round table stood neatly amongst all three.

They stood as she approached. Nathaniel smiled hesitantly, Ethan more freely. *Deep breath, Mia. All you have to do is smile, turn to Nathaniel Hamilton and say hello.* How hard could it be?

Hard.

'Hi,' she said finally, juggling her folder and belatedly holding out her hand. Should she introduce herself? She had no idea. Neither, it seemed, did Nathaniel. His handshake was brief, his eyes warm and faintly anxious.

'Dad, this is Mia. Mia—my father, Nathaniel,' said Ethan into the silence, and it was done. That first wobbly baby step towards her goal. Ethan saw her seated, and with a glance had a waiter hurrying over to take her order.

'Gin and tonic.' Her words shook alarmingly. So much for cool and confident. 'And water. One of each. And ice. Ice on the side. Thank you.'

'Certainly, madam,' said the waiter, and disappeared.

'What did I just order?' she whispered to Ethan as they sat down.

'Beats me. Relax. It's just a drink.'

Right. She took a deep breath, let it out slowly. Oh, God, what now? She slid Ethan another glance, only to find him watching her closely. *Say something,* she pleaded silently. *Don't make me carry this conversation because I can't do it. I'll say the wrong thing and ruin everything and I don't want to.* Now that she was sitting here with Ethan's father, Lily's partner of twenty-four years, she desperately wanted to like him—and for him to like her.

And then Ethan was leaning over her, sliding Sanjay's quote from her nerveless fingers and setting it on the table as he gave her a smile he usually reserved for the bedroom. 'Relax,' he muttered. 'Think of the gym in an hour's time.'

'Not helping,' she muttered, sliding a hurried glance in Nathaniel's direction. His expression was noncommittal, but his eyes missed nothing.

'He always was a law unto himself,' said Nathaniel gently, and, glancing at the folder, 'I hear you've found an interior decorator of rare and discerning talent.'

'Did Ethan tell you that?'

Nathaniel smiled as his focus shifted to Ethan. 'Perhaps not in those exact words.'

'Ethan's a little short on vision when it comes to soft furnishings,' she said as Ethan eased back into his chair and grinned at her. 'Brilliant architect and project manager, though.' Grudgingly she gave the devil his due. Ethan's grin widened.

'You should ask him to take you on a tour of our

other hotels when you've finished here,' said Nathaniel. 'Some of them are quite superb.'

'Yes, well…' She didn't know what Ethan's plans were after they'd finished the Cornwallis, but she doubted they involved him and her jaunting round the world's luxury hotels together. 'I'll probably have my hands full getting the hotel running smoothly after that.'

'You're not going to appoint a manager?' asked Nathaniel.

'Eventually,' she conceded. 'But not yet. I think I'm going to like this business of running a hotel.'

'Careful, Mia,' said Ethan. 'It's addictive.'

'Besides,' she said on a more serious note, 'I have shareholders to answer to. I promised them a return on their investment. I need to make good.'

Nathaniel looked uncomfortable. Ethan picked up the drink in front of him and sipped it. 'You will.'

'So what will *you* do after we finish the Cornwallis?' she asked curiously. 'Business as usual?'

'Maybe not straight away.' Ethan looked at his father. 'I've finished the plans for the beach house,' he said quietly. 'This time I thought I might build it.'

Mia looked from one man to the other, sensing a depth to this conversation she couldn't decipher. But Ethan didn't elaborate and she wasn't about to ask. Not in front of his father at any rate.

'Ethan's been planning this beach house since he was a boy,' Nathaniel told her. 'He found the land a few years back and I thought he might build it then, but he never did.' And, to Ethan, 'I could stay on a while. I'd like to see you build that house, Ethan. I'd like to see you finally build a home.'

Ethan said nothing.

'Sounds like we'll all have plenty to do then,' she said brightly. 'Which brings me to another question. I've been reading up on the festival of hungry ghosts— we're having a feast for the ghost of Yuen Chin on the fifteenth,' she said to Nathaniel.

'Ethan mentioned it.'

'Yes, well…' She ploughed ahead before she lost her nerve altogether. 'Apparently the night before that is often reserved for a smaller, more intimate celebration. A meal where family get together to honour their ancestors. And seeing as I never made it here in time for Lily's funeral…' She clenched her hands tightly around the edge of the chair. 'I was wondering if you would join me for a meal. Both of you. In Lily's honour.'

'I'd be honoured to attend,' said Nathaniel.

'Ethan?' She eyed him anxiously, sensing his hesitation and not quite knowing where it had come from.

'I'll be there,' he said gruffly.

'Good.' *Deep breath, Mia.* 'I've also invited another guest. He hasn't accepted yet, but I'm hoping he will. I'm hoping his presence won't be a problem for either of you.' Her voice wobbled alarmingly but her resolve stayed firm. 'I've invited my father.'

'That's as it should be,' said Nathaniel, after a long, long, pause. 'I hope he accepts your invitation.'

Talk turned to soft furnishings and fabrics after that, led by Nathaniel as he leafed through Sanjay's proposal.

'Beautiful,' he said. 'Original. Lily would have loved it. Not all of it, however, is entirely practical. Not when it comes to cleaning and maintaining a high occupancy rate hotel.'

Mia leaned forward in her seat as Nathaniel turned the folder towards her so she could view it right way up. 'I suggest using tougher fabrics here,' he said. 'And you'll need darker coloured carpet or replaceable runners in these high-volume areas here.'

Mia nodded.

'What about the runner for the grand staircase?' murmured Ethan. 'Show him that one.'

Mia did, and held her breath. Nathaniel looked at it, looked at her. Sighed. 'It's perfect.'

'Hear that?' she said to Ethan. 'It's perfect.'

Ethan looked at his father incredulously. Nathan smiled wryly. 'A piece of advice from an old man, son. Some battles you're simply going to lose. Move on.'

The hour passed quickly as talk turned to Penang and the changes the island had seen over the years.

Mia's water glass stood empty. So did her gin and tonic glass. Her ice on the side—in a small silver bucket with tongs alongside it—had melted, but she refused another drink. So did Nathaniel, telling her he had a mah-jong engagement with an old acquaintance.

'I wondered,' he said hesitantly as they prepared to leave, 'if I might leave you with a small gift.' He drew a clumsily wrapped parcel from beside his chair and held it towards her. A box of chocolates, maybe? It was about the right size. Perhaps a box of sweets?

'I… Thank you,' she said, sensing that it was important to him that she accept it. She took it, slipped her finger beneath the tape.

'Don't open it *now!*' he said hurriedly.

Uh-oh. Not chocolates.

'Open it later,' he continued. 'When you get to your room.'

Mia smiled. She couldn't help it. 'I'll be in touch about those dinner arrangements.'

Nathaniel nodded. 'It's been a pleasure meeting you, Mia Fletcher.'

'Yes,' she said. 'Yes. It's good to meet you, too.'

Ethan prowled Mia's room once they reached it. Edgy, restless, as she slipped off her shoes and set the parcel down on the bed. The meeting had gone ahead, and gone well. His father was happy. Mia was happy. He should be happy.

He wasn't.

'What's wrong?' asked Mia, more attuned to him than he wanted her to be.

'Nothing.' Nothing he could put his finger on.

'I will concede that the grand staircase runner is a luxury,' she said after a moment. 'One that may well need a rethink on account of budget constraints.'

'It's not that.'

Mia's gaze went to the parcel on the bed. Ethan's followed.

'There's something in that parcel you'd rather I didn't have?'

Ethan sighed, ran a hand through his hair. 'I have no idea what's in the parcel, Mia. I don't care. Whatever it is was willingly given. It's yours now.'

'So…what's wrong?'

'Nothing. Open the parcel.'

Now it was Mia's turn for restlessness as she shuffled papers from on top of chairs to the desk so he could sit. He didn't want to sit. 'I'm not sure I want to open it,' she admitted finally. 'Last time I opened a mystery envelope I cried for a week.'

'I thought you'd *want* to see some photos of your mother,' he said defensively.

'I did. I still cried for a week.'

He leaned back against the desk and stared at the parcel.

Mia perched next to him, arms crossed tightly around her waist as she did the same. 'You open it,' she said.

'Me?' Ethan shook his head. 'He gave it to you.'

'Yes, but you could be the advance scout—sensing danger and warning the fair maiden that there be trouble ahead.'

'Your hair is black, Mia.'

'Picky, picky.' She sighed, and kept right on staring at the parcel.

'I'm proud of you,' he said quietly.

'Thank you.' A smile flittered about her lips. 'I'm proud of me, too.'

'You think your father will come around?'

'I phoned him this morning. Sent a handwritten invite on embossed Cornwallis Hotel paper to him by international courier this afternoon. Tomorrow I'll send him a plane ticket.'

'And the day after that?'

'The day after that I'll play hardball and send him that picture Lily took of him when the elephant pit collapsed. The one with him looking up at her and laughing.'

'Ouch.' Ethan rubbed at his heart through the cotton of his shirt. 'That one's going to hurt.'

'Not as much as the next one. I'm thinking of sending him one of the ones you took of me at work.'

'Which one?'

'The one when we raised the chandelier in the foyer and first turned it on.'

She stood and walked towards the parcel, circled it. 'Well, we know it's not a fur coat,' she said finally.

'True,' he said. 'Who'd wear fur in this climate?'

'Do you think it's something of hers?'

'It's a distinct possibility.'

'Hopefully not a photo album,' she muttered. 'Did she keep a diary?'

'Not that I know of.' He eyed the parcel speculatively. 'Could be jewellery.'

'Uh-oh,' said Mia.

'You don't like jewellery?'

'I do like jewellery,' she assured him. 'But if this is jewellery and it belonged to my mother there *will* be tears.'

He thought as much. 'Well, that's me, then,' he said. 'Gotta go. Things to do.'

'Coward,' she muttered absently. 'You want my body later, you can put up with a few tears now. Did she have a lot of jewellery?'

Ethan debated the pros and cons of tears versus mind-bending sex, figured he could withstand a few tears after all. 'A few pieces. Not that many.' He smiled. 'She had a garden instead.'

'Well,' said Mia, finally picking up the parcel. 'It's not a garden.'

'Also true.'

He watched and waited as the paper came off to reveal a red velvet jewellery box. Ethan had seen it before. He scanned the room; the tissues were by the bed. That was handy.

'It's a locket,' she said in a small voice.

Ethan nodded and his eyes met hers. He knew the one. A small oval locket, very plain, very old. Made of gold. He knew what was in it—knew what she'd see. A tiny lock of fine black hair tied together with a scrap of white ribbon. 'Open it.'

She did, and again her gaze sought his. 'Whose hair is this?' Mia's voice was hardly more than a choked whisper.

'It's yours.' He waited gingerly, expecting tears, but there were no tears—just big grey eyes filled with strength and quiet peace.

'Will you help me put it on?'

'Later,' he said, as he drew her into his arms and his lips met hers. Later.

Mia trembled as Ethan's kiss swept through her. The quick slick slide of heat and fire, the burning need for more. He gave unstintingly as passion rolled through them. Passion and strength mixed with patience and understanding. He gave without thinking, without knowing how it would bind her to him. He didn't call it love—no, he wouldn't call it that.

Only she called it that.

Ethan shuddered as Mia's lips opened beneath his own. He'd tasted her passion, knew it as intimately as his own, but this time, in this place, she offered something more. Tenderness. He felt it, returned it, sliding her hair from her face with gentle fingers. Sweetness as she stood before him defenceless, her eyes unguarded, promising everything—everything and more.

He closed his eyes because he didn't want to see—didn't want to know what it was she offered so freely. But he didn't let her go. Instead he sank into another kiss and drove the flames higher. Giving what he could. Hoping it would be enough. Knowing it wasn't. He'd warned her. He *had* warned her.

'You give too much,' he muttered.

'Worry about your own heart,' she said, and her kisses changed, gentleness forgotten in the face of a need so fierce and true it took his breath away.

They made it to the bed. Made it out of their clothes. He reached for her, reared over her, darkly pleased when she arched into him and her eyes glazed over with passion. This much he could give her—this blind, relentless pleasure. It was enough.

He would make it enough.

Later, much later, Ethan lay on his side next to a sleeping Mia. The diffused light of the city by night filtered in through the windows, casting shadows in corners and gilding the rest of the room. His body was sated, relaxed, content.

And still sleep eluded him.

She was getting too close. Slipping beneath his defences. She'd made peace with his father. Hell, he'd encouraged it—not realising that by doing so she would inch that much closer to his heart, making him admire her courage in staring at the past with honest eyes, accepting it, and moving on. Making him care.

He didn't want to care.

He glanced towards her, planning retreat, only to find her watching him through sleepy, satisfied eyes. Her lips were still faintly swollen from his onslaught, and her skin glowed like porcelain. She looked wanton, well loved. Infinitely dangerous.

'Hey,' she said, with the hint of a smile. 'You want to share a few of those black thoughts?'

'Not really.'

She grabbed for a pillow they'd cast aside earlier and

propped it under her head. 'May I ask you a personal question?'

'Has *no* ever stopped you?'

'How come you never built your beach house?'

He rolled onto his back and tucked a hand under his head as he stared at the ceiling. 'For a long time I didn't have the land.'

'But you found land eventually?'

'Yeah.' Arianne had found it, on her way to God only knew where. Half-wild and all wrong, she'd told him laughingly. Just like her. Beautiful, though. He'd gone to look at it and fallen in love with the sweeping ocean view. Bought it without even bothering to haggle over the price.

'Why didn't you build it then?'

'I just never got around to it.'

'Because your wife died?'

'No.'

'You never talk about her, Ethan.'

He wasn't about to start.

'The other day you helped paint a picture of my past that I could deal with. You encouraged me to look forward, not back. I'd like to think I could do the same for you.'

'I do look forward.'

'Then how come you never let anyone close to you?'

'You're close,' he muttered. 'You're right here.'

'And I'm still nowhere near you. What happened to her, Ethan? What did she do to you? What happened to make you so afraid of your feelings?'

'Nothing.' He didn't want to talk about it. Not with Mia. Not with anyone. He sat up, rolled over to the edge of the bed and reached for the clothes he'd tossed aside earlier. 'I have to go.'

Mia sighed heavily. 'You're *supposed* to reveal all. I'm supposed to help you see it from a different perspective. And then you heal.'

'Why? So I can fall headlong in love with you?' He was mortally afraid that he already had. 'It's not going to happen, Mia.' He jerked his trousers on, slid her a dark glance. 'This is who I am. I've already given you all I have to give. Take it or leave it.'

Mia's eyes were on his. Thoughtful. Measuring.

'I'll think about it,' she said.

CHAPTER TEN

MIA thought about Ethan's ultimatum over the next few days. He kept his distance and she kept busy: a mutual reassessment of their situation which one way or another would have to end soon. She could dither with the best when she was undecided on something, but it wasn't indecision that stayed her tongue on this. She knew what she wanted; the knowledge burned into her soul. There would be no other love for her. Not in this lifetime. Only Ethan. And only on his terms.

It was almost enough.

She was stuck. Gloriously, heart-wrenchingly stuck. Because walking away from him was impossible and he wasn't about to surrender his heart. So she waited. And she thought about it.

She gave Sanjay the go-ahead to decorate the north wing apartment, and together they chose the furniture that would go in it. She arranged a feast for at least one hungry ghost, and an army of workmen and their extended families. She sent ruthlessly sentimental reminders to her father that his presence was requested on the fourteenth day of the seventh lunar month. If her father thought she'd relent, he was mistaken.

And if Ethan thought he could drive her away with

tough talk of taking what he wanted and giving nothing back, *he* was mistaken. He gave without knowing. Gave her everything she'd ever wanted. Steadfast support for her business goals. Never once had he said, "Don't do it, don't dream." He'd rolled up his sleeves and dreamed right along with her, and together they'd dreamed big. And he'd shown gentle understanding of the demons that plagued her. He'd *known* she wouldn't rest until she knew what had driven her parents to do what they had. He'd helped her understand the decisions they'd made. Helped her accept them. Forgive them.

He was generous with his time, generous with his knowledge.

Overwhelmingly generous with his body.

As for his reluctance to talk about his wife—well, maybe they could work on that. Because she hadn't given up.

She never gave up on the people she loved.

'What do you think?'

Mia stood before him, hands on hips, her eyes alight with laughter, having just dragged him through the door of her newly refurbished apartment.

Ethan thought she looked more staggeringly beautiful than ever. He hadn't held her in days. Trying to act the gentleman rather than the marauder. Trying to give her the space to make a decision about their relationship without the distraction of mind-bending sex.

'Ethan, you're not even looking!'

Ethan rubbed his forehead, pretty sure she meant that he wasn't looking around the apartment. 'I'm not sure I'm game.'

Ayah had been up to see the interior earlier in the

day and had returned wearing a wide and toothy grin. Rajah had gone up next and come back down shaking his head. Lady Eleanora Jolie had seen it as a work in progress two days ago, telling Ethan when she popped into his makeshift office to say hello that she'd enlisted Sanjay to do her house next. She was eighty-two next month, she'd told him. She needed a raunchy bedroom boudoir before she ran out of time. Tastefully done, of course.

Of course.

'You do know that the only person you have to please is *you?*' he said quietly.

'I love it when you say that. Sadly, where the rest of the hotel is concerned I have the paying public and a parcel of shareholders to think about as well. I trust your judgement,' she said with a wry smile. 'I need your opinion. Your honest one.'

'You'll get it,' he warned her and, preparing for the worst, turned his attention to the room. After Lady Jolie's raunchy boudoir comment he'd been expecting clashing garish colours more suited to a marketplace than a luxury hotel, but this was sophisticated old-world elegance enhanced by the colours of the Orient. Warm, welcoming, spacious and soothing. 'It's good,' he said, after close examination of the dining room and the sunroom, the kitchen and the lounge. 'Very good.'

'So you think we should let Sanjay loose on the rest of the hotel?'

Ethan nodded.

'Excellent. Consider it done. Of course he has a treasure trove of beautiful pieces to work with,' she said, running her hand along the back of a dining room chair. 'Most of the stuff Lily had in here is back.'

'Most of the stuff Lily had in here was handed down through your father's family.'

'Oh.' She paused to consider the notion. 'Even better.' And, with a decidedly wicked grin, 'Wait 'til you see the bedroom. I have a mirror framed by soaring bronze dragons. It's the size of a house. And silk-clad window seats and jewel-coloured cushions. And then there's the bed—a huge four-poster bed just begging to be misused.'

Ethan cleared his throat. 'Later.'

'I'm moving in this afternoon,' she said. 'And at seven-thirty tonight I'm having seafood Laksa, a moderately sweet white wine, and hopefully you. Not in any particular order. I'm mentioning this because according to our guidelines you need to agree to tonight being a mutually convenient time and here being a mutually convenient place.'

There had to be a catch. 'So…you've thought about it? The taking or leaving it thing?'

'Indeed I have.'

'And?' he asked gruffly.

'I'm taking it.' She stepped closer, trailed her fingers down his chest. 'Whatever you can give, for as long as you intend to give it.'

'Some people would call that surrender,' he muttered, even as his lips descended on hers, ravenously hungry, painfully needy.

'They'd be wrong,' she whispered breathlessly when at last he broke their kiss. 'There is one condition, though, Ethan.'

'What is it?' he muttered, willing to give her almost anything. He'd missed her so much.

'I want you to tell me about your wife.'

* * *

Ethan made it to Mia's just after eight that evening. Not deliberately late, no. But there'd been a double-booking of one of the Hamilton's function rooms, his events manager was down with the flu, and he'd stayed to sort it out. He let himself in the side entrance and made his way to the north wing, past the recently completed spa and hot pool complex. The water had gone into the pool two days ago. Better to find out if something wasn't quite right now rather than after he'd signed off on the work. Everything was working perfectly so far, except for the inlet valve on the smaller of the two spa pools, which had a habit of springing open at random and filling the spa. The plumbers had replaced the valve twice so far, the second time with a pre-tested valve in perfect working order, and still the spa continued to fill at random.

The plumbers were adamant.

It was Yuen Chin's doing.

He knocked on the door when he got to the apartment, not quite knowing what to expect. He'd dressed casually. Grey trousers, white linen shirt with the sleeves rolled to his elbows, collar, no tie. Much the same as what he wore in his own apartment of an evening. Mia had a habit of unbuttoning his shirt over the course of an evening. He had a habit of letting her.

She opened the door to him, casually barefoot. The rest of her appearance just about stopped his breath. She wore a pale pink halter-neck silk sundress that stopped well short of her knees. The neckline dipped low, those thin little straps no deterrent at all to someone who wanted to feast on her.

'You're here,' she said, with a very feminine smile. 'I thought you'd changed your mind.'

He nearly had. He still might. 'I had a small problem at the Hamilton to see to.'

'Hmm.' She turned around and walked inside, leaving him to follow. The dress seemed to be missing a back, dipping to her waist, exposing an abundance of porcelain skin. His gaze skidded to the sleek curves of her bottom. Invisible underwear? Or none?

He followed her, expecting that she would lead him through to the kitchen, expecting informality because that was what he was used to with her. But she led him through to the dining room instead, bare feet making no sound on the polished wooden floor as she made her way past the cabinet full of porcelain dolls, past the photos on the wall towards the dining table. Two tapered white candles stood waiting to be lit. White linen napkins sat waiting to be unfolded alongside polished silverware and fine white china. 'Are we celebrating something?'

'No, we're practising for dinner on the fourteenth. Too formal, do you think?'

'No.'

'Oh, good.' She pulled out a chair for him. Her raised eyebrow told him she expected him to sit. He did. Warily. 'Thank you.'

'You're welcome. Wine?' She plucked a bottle of white wine from a silver ice bucket and perched on the edge of the table, her dress riding way, way up her thigh as she leaned over to pour him a glass.

'No, thank you.'

She poured one for him anyway, her movements deft and self-assured, her smile innocent as she put the bottle back on ice. She put her fingertip to a wayward drop of wine sliding down the side of the bottle and then put it to her mouth, deliberately drawing attention to seemingly unpainted lips and shapely nails. She *could* have been wearing lipstick, of course. Maybe she'd just applied it so subtly it could hardly be seen. Hard to say. It was just like his deliberations on her current underwear status.

Inconclusive.

Her nails, however, were a vibrant screaming red, and she drew them away from her lips almost reluctantly. He wanted *his* fingers on her lips, right before he coaxed her mouth open to accept his kiss. He was almost certain she knew it.

This wasn't just dinner.

This was war.

She slid from the table and disappeared into the kitchen, reappearing moments later with two steaming bowls of food. She set one in front of him, her breasts brushing his shoulder, before taking her seat at the opposite end of the table. 'Wait. Mustn't forget to light the candles.' A taper burned softly on the sideboard. Mia fetched it, stretching across the big wooden table to reach the candles she'd placed dead centre.

'Allow me,' he said, moving behind her, deliberately running his fingers along her arm before closing his hand over hers. He hadn't touched her in three days and his body knew it. *Her* body knew it, too, if the sudden smouldering glance she gave him was any indication.

'Thank you.' She drew her hand out from beneath his, blew out the taper, and swiftly slipped away.

'My pleasure.' He sat back down, shook his napkin out and dropped it over his lap. 'Have you heard from your father lately?'

'Mmm. He sent me a fax.'

He picked up his fork and dug in. 'What did it say?'

Mia's lips curved. '"I surrender."'

Ethan swallowed hard on his mouthful of food, refusing to feel intimidated by her success. 'I'm impressed.'

'You should be. How's the food?'

'Delicious.' He dug his fork in for more. He might even manage to taste it this time. Mia trailed slim scarlet-tipped fingers up the stem of her wineglass and lifted it to her lips. Nope.

'I forgot the music,' she murmured.

'We *don't* need music,' he countered. The rapid thudding of his heart was enough.

'What about on the fourteenth. Do you think we'll need music then?'

'I don't know, Mia. I think you're going to have to play that one as it comes.' Her gaze slid briefly to the photo of him, his father and her father on the beach. 'They were childhood friends once; they probably still have a lot in common.'

'Yeah,' she said. But she didn't sound convinced.

'Second thoughts about bringing them together?'

'A few.' She smiled wryly. 'Sanjay will kill me if I get blood on the Persian.'

'You're asking a lot of your father, Mia.'

'I know,' she said. 'I'm thinking of asking more. I'm thinking of asking everyone to follow Chinese tradition and bring a paper gift. A gift for Lily in the afterlife. Given freely, from the heart.'

'You're asking him to forgive her?'

'It's time.' Her knowing grey eyes never left his face. 'Feel free to bring something along for *your* ghosts as well.'

'An ounce of forgiveness, you mean?'

'Or a pound of flesh. Whatever's easier.'

He smiled at that. Reluctantly. 'Don't push me, Mia.'

'By asking about your wife? You could always just tell me what I want to know. Then it'd be done.'

'There's no *need* for you to know.'

'You know *so* little about women.'

'It's not a pretty story.'

'I'm not expecting one.' She sat there waiting, her expression faintly grim. 'I'm playing by your rules, Ethan. I deserve to know why you made them.'

She had a point. But he didn't know where to start. He'd never spoken about Arianne. Not to anyone.

'I fell in love with Arianne the moment I saw her,' he said roughly. 'Fell hard. Within a month we were married. Within three months our marriage was in trouble. I gave her what I could, but it was never enough. She always had to have more. More clothes, more time, more…men. She told me it was because I always held back. That if she couldn't have all of me she'd have everything else instead.'

'You think you're to blame for her taking lovers?'

'I couldn't give her what she needed.'

'Perhaps no one could?'

'I kept a piece of me back.'

Mia said nothing.

'I stayed with her,' he continued. 'Loved her as best I could.' He smiled mirthlessly. 'Hated her. And then one day she stumbled across a heart as wild and unfettered as her own. She took it, toyed with it, wielding love like a weapon. Playing him, playing me, until I couldn't see the sky for darkness.' He took a deep breath. 'I told her I wanted out. That it was me or him.

And she laughed and said that she'd do what she liked and that she'd damn well have us both.'

Mia closed her eyes, a tear spilling from beneath her lashes to trail down her cheek. But Ethan was beyond stopping. She'd wanted to know about Arianne, she could damn well listen. Grief slammed into him, and rage for what he'd endured, guilt for what he'd never been able to give. None of it was Mia's fault, not one bit of it, and still he lashed out at her. 'You want to know how Arianne died, Mia? Right there, down on that beach, with her lover's hands around her neck as he held her under. He killed her in rage, and a day later he killed himself. Part of me wept for her,' he said savagely. 'But not all. Not all. I hated myself. And by God I hated her. It almost destroyed me.'

'Ethan—'

'No!' So much for dinner. He stood abruptly, clumsy in his haste to escape the memories that piled in on him. 'I'm sorry,' he said, as Mia stared back at him white-faced, little more than a ghost herself. 'But I can't fall in love with you, Mia. I won't. I can't go through that again. Not even for you.'

Mia sat motionless as the door slammed shut behind him, her head bowed, her hands tightly clasped in her lap to stop them from trembling. 'You wouldn't have to,' she whispered brokenly as a cool breeze swept in from the ocean, setting the napkins to fluttering and the candles to flickering. 'You wouldn't have to.'

CHAPTER ELEVEN

RICHARD FLETCHER arrived in Georgetown, Penang, on the morning of the fourteenth day of August. Mia was waiting for him.

She watched as he cleared the airport arrivals doors, a dark-haired, handsome man with eyes of bleakest grey. He looked remote and forbidding—but then he always had. When he smiled—and that was rare—his face took on an unexpected sweetness that warmed a person through.

He saw her.

And he smiled.

'Daughter,' he said gruffly when he reached her.

'Daddy,' she said, fighting back the tears, and then she was in his arms. 'How long can you stay?'

'A week. Maybe. My new PA isn't as knowledgeable as my old one.' He drew back to look at her. 'I don't suppose you'd consider coming back?'

Mia shook her head and softened her reply with a smile. 'I love it here,' she said simply.

'Penang suits you. I always knew it would. When this place takes hold it's hard to shake.' His eyes narrowed as he searched her face. 'You look tired.'

'I've been busy.' Nothing to do with hardly having

slept since Ethan had walked out of her apartment and stayed out. 'The hotel's almost finished. The refurbishment work is complete. Now it's just a matter of cleaning and furnishing the interior. Come, I'll show you.'

Rajah stood waiting at the door as they arrived, resplendent in the bone-coloured tunic and turban, never mind that that they weren't even open for business yet. Mia hadn't asked him to. He'd dressed that way of his own accord. Ayah, dressed in her daytime finest, stood next to him.

'Mr Richard,' said Rajah. 'It's good to see you.' For once his sentence contained no polysyllabic words.

'Rajah,' said her father, with another of his rare smiles, and they shook hands. Then his gaze switched to Ayah. 'Ayah,' he said quietly, and gathered her in his arms as her tears started to fall.

'You're back,' she said as she clung to him. 'You're back.' And launched into a barrage of Tamil.

'You've been looking after my girl?' he said, when finally she released him.

'You know I have.' Ayah offered up a glare through her tears. 'Why you not come sooner?'

'It doesn't matter,' said Mia firmly. 'He's here now. He's here for a week.' And, to her father, 'I've refurbished the north wing apartment. I live there now. You can stay with me, or you can stay in the penthouse suite. Same floor, east wing. Sanjay and his team worked day and night to get it ready for you, just in case.'

'Sanjay?'

'Our former window-measurer, now turned interior decorator, currently enjoying the rather precarious honour of being Madame Sari's favourite son-in-law. It's a long story. One he'll no doubt tell you all about if you ever meet him.' Mia grinned. 'He's obscenely talented. It wouldn't hurt to keep him in mind for some of Fletcher Corp's future projects.'

Her father nodded absently as he glanced around the foyer. The last of the tradesmen were pulling out today, along with the last of the tools, planks, drop cloths and leftover building materials. The foyer was in chaos, but a careful eye could see what had been done. The marble was carefully relevelled and polished to a high gloss, the staircase balustrades stripped back to reveal the glorious wood grain, then oiled and polished to a subtle gleam. The chandelier sparkled from its perch high above them, the ceilings gleamed white, and the walls added a touch of barely-there green.

The bones were there, and they were everything Mia had dreamed they'd be. Everything and more.

Her father's gaze halted abruptly when it reached the reception desk. Mia looked to see what had captured his attention so completely.

Ethan.

She hadn't seen him in two days. Her father hadn't seen him in twenty-four years. 'That's Ethan,' she said huskily.

'I know,' her father said simply.

He came over to them, his gaze oddly searching as it met hers, before he turned his attention to her father. 'Richard,' he said, holding out his hand. 'Welcome back. It's been a long time.'

'So it has.' Her father shook hands. 'Mia tells me you've been managing the bulk of the restoration work. Thank you for helping her.'

'I promised Lily I would,' he said, and sent an arrow straight to her heart.

'I'd like to think it hasn't always been an act of duty for you,' she said quietly. 'I'd like to think you helped because you wanted to. Because you enjoyed bringing the hotel to life just as much as I did.'

He glanced at her, and just as quickly looked away, as if it hurt to look at her. 'The paperwork's in order. Everyone's been paid. I'll finish up this afternoon with the rest of the subcontractors.' The arrow twisted, tearing as it went. 'It's all yours.'

She tried to smile in the face of Ethan's cool indifference, but couldn't quite manage it. She settled for not weeping instead, and tried to think of business. 'Except for the forty-five per cent belonging to shareholders. Which makes it only mostly mine.'

Ethan shared a glance with her father. Both men looked uncomfortable. Perhaps they were uncomfortable with each other.

Or perhaps there was another reason.

Mia stared from one man to the other, noticing not for the first time the similarities between them. The aloofness they wore like a shield, their closely guarded hearts. Their words were all business, but every now and then…every now and then their actions betrayed them. 'Anything either of you want to tell me?'

Her father shook his head.

'Can't think of anything,' said Ethan blandly.

Hmm. 'If you're holding those shares, Ethan, I'll skewer you alive.'

'You can try.' The flash of fire in his eyes was better than cool and heartbreaking indifference. Much, much better. 'You turned them loose to the public, Mia. You get what you get and you live with it.'

'So do you have them or not?'

'There is something I need to tell you,' he said abruptly. 'I'm heading to Malacca this afternoon. I doubt I'll be able to make it back in time for dinner.'

She should have expected it. Ethan was nothing if not thorough. He didn't love her. He didn't *want* to love her. His withdrawal would be complete. But damned if he could stop her loving him.

'I'll set a place for you anyway,' she told him. Just in case.

Mia saw her father settled in the penthouse suite, and set Rajah to showing him around the hotel. She'd have done it herself, except that something stretched between her father, Rajah and Ayah—something unexpected and true. A bond of old, of friendship and of love. She could see it in the way Rajah's wizened gaze rested on her father. See it in Ayah's fussing.

Her father had come because she'd asked him. Because she'd badgered and coerced him and given him little choice. He'd come because he loved her, for all that the words remained unspoken, but there was more to his coming here than that. She'd been so focussed on herself and on Lily that she'd missed it.

Richard Fletcher had come home.

She cornered Ayah the minute her father and Rajah started out on their tour of the hotel. 'What food did he like as a boy? What were his favourites?' She had a feeling Ayah would know.

Ayah *did* know, and threw herself into the collection of ingredients and the supplying of recipes wholeheartedly. An hour later they were in Mia's kitchen, surrounded by exotic foods and spices. Mia had no idea what half of them were, but they smelled divine, and under Ayah's guidance she figured out what to do with them. The dragon fruit, with its smooth and vibrant pink skin and yellow-tipped scales, needed to be chilled in the fridge and cut just before serving. She'd find white flesh shot through with tiny edible black seeds in it, Ayah assured her. To be put on a plate and served with a spoon.

They diced tiny fresh chillis, ground up spices and ginger, and when the paste hit the pan the air filled with the scent that Mia had come to think of as uniquely Penang. Her eyes watered with the strength of the chilli and the overflow of emotion. They made lamb curry from scratch, and added cucumber to a bowl of freshly made yoghurt. They made pumpkin and coriander cubes and mango chutney, dough for the roti, and a fish soup the likes of which Mia had never seen.

'He was always in my kitchen as a boy,' said Ayah, her eyes soft. 'Or somewhere in the grounds with Rajah. Bananas in coconut!' she said suddenly. 'You'll need to chop them just before serving.'

Mia nodded and tossed three bananas and a packet of shredded coconut into a bowl and put it to one side. 'Bananas in coconut. Check.'

'Not that your grandparents were bad people,' said Ayah, shooting her a glance. 'They just didn't know what to do with a child. Always too busy off somewhere else. And then...' Ayah picked up a large knife and began slicing beans. 'Both of them dead, just like that, and your father barely a man.'

Killed in a plane crash. Mia knew that much and not a lot more.

'Your father grew up lonely, my Mia. When he met

your mother he gave her his heart. Such a tender heart.'
Ayah shook her head. 'Such a loyal one.'

'You do know who's coming to this dinner party?'
said Mia hesitantly. 'Nathaniel and my father and...
Ethan. You know who it's for?'

Ayah nodded.

'Am I asking too much of them, Ayah? Am I asking
the impossible?'

'I don't know, child.' Ayah stared back at her, her face
creased with lines and her eyes heavy with the wisdom
of age. 'But ask it anyway.'

At six-thirty exactly, Mia stopped fussing with the
food, the wine selection and the table preparations,
and started to prepare herself for the evening ahead. A
simple black dress—not sexy, not plain. A black dress
for mourning. She put it on. And took it off, reaching
instead for a dove-grey crêpe sheath.

This wasn't about mourning. It was about remem-
brance, forgiveness, healing and moving on, and she
would not wear black for that. 'It's not just for you,
Mama. This is for all of us, and you need to help me.'
The locket went on last, and Mia stood there in front
of the mirror, her enormous dragon-edged mirror, and
her mother's face stared back at her, with her father's
eyes. 'Help me be strong.'

At seven-fifteen her father arrived, his eyes shadowed
as his gaze skittered over the locket she wore at her
throat. He handed her a bottle of wine in silence. 'Thank
you,' she said quietly. 'Thank you for coming.'

At precisely seven-thirty Nathaniel Hamilton arrived. Alone. He had orchids for her, sweets for the

table, quiet, wary eyes, and a handshake for her father. 'Welcome home,' he said to her father. 'Welcome home.'

She poured wine for them both, from the bottle she'd opened earlier. Poured a glass for herself. The table was set, the food ready to serve. They were here. All of them here.

Except Ethan.

She waited fifteen more minutes. Hoping he'd come. Filling the long silences with small talk that centred around the hotel renovations and earning for her efforts a comment from her father here, a word from Nathaniel there.

'It's not like Ethan to be late,' said Nathaniel, as Mia glanced at the clock for the tenth time in as many minutes.

'He wasn't sure he could make it,' she said carefully. 'But he might. Are you hungry? How hungry are you?'

They waited another fifteen minutes before Mia finally put them to work filling the table with the food she and Ayah had prepared earlier. More and more dishes, until the table groaned beneath their weight. A smile tilted the corners of her father's lips as he stared at the table. His eyes sought hers.

'Ayah and I did a little cooking this afternoon,' she said, deliberately offhand. 'Sit, please. Both of you. And eat.'

Music. She'd forgotten the music. And this time they needed it. Mellow and easy, to fill the silences and relax the mind. She hesitated on her way around the table. She should take the fourth setting away. It would make more room on the table for everything else. But her heart held to the hope that Ethan would still come. That he'd been held up at the hotel and would be here eventually. He

knew how much this meal meant to her. He'd be here.
He would. Wouldn't he?

'Call him,' said Nathaniel, his gaze troubled. '*I'll*
call him.'

'No!' She shot Nathaniel an apologetic smile to make
up for her hasty reply. 'No, it's all right. There's no
need.' She took her seat and set to playing hostess—
teasing her father about his appetite for Ayah's curry,
asking Nathaniel questions about the changes Penang
had seen in the last twenty years. Questions to ignite
dialogue between the two men, no matter how awkward
it was to begin with. They tried. They did try. But the
silences grew longer and Mia couldn't fill them. The
empty place setting opposite mocked her, reminding
her of a time when it hadn't been empty, when Ethan
had sat opposite and she'd pushed him for answers he
hadn't wanted to give.

He'd warned her, over and over, but she hadn't listened to him. She'd listened to her heart instead. Her
hand went to her locket, her eyes dry and hot. *He
warned me, Mama. He did warn me. Help me be strong.*

'I heard,' said her father, picking up the conversation, 'that you moved the Hamilton Hotel group into
China successfully?' His words were for Nathaniel, but
his eyes were on her, questioning and concerned. She
offered up a smile, glanced at Nathaniel. He was looking at her, too, only his gaze wasn't questioning. It was
sympathetic.

'Our first attempt was a disaster,' said Nathaniel con-
versationally, bestowing on her a gentle, encouraging
smile before turning his attention to the feast spread
out before them. 'But Ethan stuck it out and finally negotiated the maze of red tape. He can be very stubborn

when he wants to be. One might almost say pigheaded.'
He reached for the curry her father had already taken a
second helping of and spooned a generous portion onto
his plate. 'Curry?' he asked her.

'No, thank you.' She still had most of what she'd put
on her plate to begin with.

'I could eat some more,' said her father, and Nathaniel
loaded up his plate.

'I haven't had curry like this in twenty-four years,'
said Nathaniel. 'Remember when—' He stopped
abruptly, locking eyes with her father. After a long,
long moment, full of unspoken memories and not nearly
enough words, he looked away.

She should never have forced them together, she
thought miserably, biting her lip and concentrating on
the pain in an effort to stop her tears from falling. Some
things were best left alone.

'I remember,' said her father gruffly, as he reached
for the cucumber in yoghurt. 'I haven't either.' And,
digging his fork into the curry on his plate, 'Damn, it's
good.'

They told her stories of two boys growing up in
Penang after that. Two boys who sounded a great deal
like them, although neither of them said as much. They
made her laugh and they filled her glass with wine, and
for a time they made her forget that empty seat at the
other end of the table.

For a time.

They ate dessert standing out on the balcony, staring out at the view, and after that she filled their glasses
and her own. *Look at them, Mama. They're doing this
for me. And I'm doing it for them. And for you.* 'I'd like
to make a toast,' she said quietly. 'To family.'

To family.
To family.
You could have been here, Ethan. You should have been here, damn you.
You and your beautiful unreachable heart.

Ethan found his father in his garden, hoe in hand, chipping away at the greenery. A baby banyan tree stood nearby, its trunk just beginning to form the wavy buttresses that would creep through the garden as the tree grew bigger. The canopy provided shade from the sultry heat of the tropical sun and ideal growing conditions for a myriad of plants, including those that were not welcome.

'Are you sure it's a weed?' he asked, by way of greeting.

'It looks like grass and it's choking everything around it. It's a weed.' His father stopped hoeing and favoured him with a long, penetrating, and not altogether hospitable stare. 'We waited dinner for you last night.'

'I told Mia I wouldn't be there.'

'And she told us. We waited anyway. Where were you, Ethan? What was more important than honouring your family?'

Protecting my heart, he wanted to say. Stopping a small woman with calm grey eyes and a smile that warmed his soul from stealing it outright. He hadn't wanted to see how she handled the evening. He *knew* how she'd approach it. Blindsiding them both with warmth and hospitality. Making the evening flow smoothly with social skills born of compassion and a generosity of spirit that left him reeling.

Ethan ran a hand through his hair. 'How did it go?'

'If you'd been there you wouldn't have to ask.' His father went back to his hoeing.

'I went to Malacca,' he said gruffly. 'To look at some wooden beams for the beach house.' His excuse was pitiful, but he'd had to get far enough away from Penang so that he *couldn't* get to the dinner, even if he wanted to. If he'd stayed in Penang he'd have ended up there. And forsaken his heart in the process. 'I stayed overnight.' He tried again. 'How was it?'

'I saw a woman's heart break last night, Ethan. I watched her hold her head high and see to my comfort and to Richard's while inside she bled out for love of you.' His father kept right on hoeing, his quiet words completely at odds with the everyday task and all the more potent because of it. 'So we did what old men do when faced with something we can't fix. We talked business and other pleasantries, rediscovered common interests, and tried to chase the misery from Mia's eyes. And it worked—for a time. Lily would have been proud of us.' Nathaniel smiled tightly. 'She would not, I think, have been proud of you.'

Ethan said nothing.

Nathaniel shook his head. 'I promised myself I wouldn't interfere. That whatever problems you and Mia had were none of my business. But you love her, Ethan. I can see it in your eyes, hear it in your voice when you talk about her. And she loves you. I saw you together, and the bond between the two of you almost made me weep because I knew that finally, finally, you'd found the other half of your soul. Do you know how rare that is? How precious?

'I know Arianne hurt you, Ethan. But she wasn't

right for you, nor you for her. Not all love ends in death and hatred and guilt. I wish to God she hadn't died. I wish it for her and I wish it for you. Because maybe then you could have been free of her.'

'She's dead,' he said harshly. 'I am free of her.'

'You think she doesn't haunt you from the grave? Poisoning every thought you have on women and relationships? Poisoning what you could have with Mia?'

'I never promised Mia anything,' he said gruffly.

'Why not, Ethan?' said his father wearily. 'Why the *hell* not?'

When Ethan brooded, he did it wholeheartedly. He sat at the desk in his office at the Hamilton, pen in hand, and stared unseeingly at the paperwork in front of him, daring anyone to come through that door with a query or a complaint. Not that they would. He'd heard Cassie, his management secretary, telling the staff that if they had a problem to deal with it as best they could or come and find her, no matter where she was or what she was doing. Today the chain of command stopped short of Ethan—unless anyone felt like losing his or her job, in which case they should go right on in and disturb the boss.

He'd have to give her a raise.

'Hey, Cassie. Ethan in?' The words were spoken in a warm and feminine voice underpinned with steel. Mia.

'He's in.' Cassie knew Mia from her time here as a guest. Mia had made a point of getting to know all the people on his payroll, from the cleaning staff up. 'But, Mia, he's in a filthy mood. I really don't think—'

'Don't worry, Cassie, we're family. I will see his

black mood and raise him a temper tantrum. Stick around. It'll be fun.'

His door opened and Mia stood there, the air fairly crackling around her. Cassie stood behind her, wringing her hands. 'Mia to see you, sir,' she said weakly.

'Take a tea break, Cassie.'

'I was thinking about taking a slow boat to the mainland.'

'Good idea,' said Mia. 'Take the company expense card with you. Stay the weekend, check out the competition. Spend liberally, and don't bother with anything below five and a half stars.'

'Half an hour, Cassie.'

'You'll let me know when you have a vacancy coming up?' Cassie said to Mia.

'See me tomorrow.' Mia closed the door behind her and turned to face him.

'Pirate,' he muttered.

'I learned from the best.' She walked towards him, past the empty chair on the other side of his desk, to perch next to him. Short, tight skirt, long, smooth legs, and a smile a sensible man would run from. 'I believe you have something of mine?'

'I guess that makes us about even, considering that soon you're going to have all my employees.'

She leaned forward and kissed him on the lips, just a whisper of a kiss that nonetheless managed to sear his soul and set his pulse to leaping. She sat back. Sighed. 'Yep, you've still got it.'

'Your undivided attention? That's because you seemed to have ticked off everything else on your to-do list. Renovating the hotel, reconciling your past, forging a family.' He sat back in his black leather office chair, seeking distance. Not finding it. 'You need a new list.'

'My heart, Ethan.' She eyed him darkly.

'Well,' he said slowly. 'You could always take it back.'

'There you go again,' she said. 'Thinking like a man. Fact is I don't *want* to take it back. I'm simply here to tell you that you have it. Just in case there was any doubt.'

Not a lot a man could say to that. Ethan decided silence wouldn't hurt at this point. Mia was spoiling for a fight. He was halfway inclined to give her one.

Silence at this point was downright necessary.

She moved closer, her skirt slid higher. 'I'm sorry your first wife hurt you so badly. I'm sorry you can't forgive her. But if you think I'm anything like her you're mistaken. Because I would *never* betray you the way she did, Ethan. I'd stand with you, loving you until the end of time, and if you can't see that then you're a fool! I'm honest, hard-working, extremely loyal, independently wealthy, tolerably attractive, and completely and irreversibly in love with you. I can also—' and here she gave a toss of her head '—reduce you to putty in the bedroom. Fortunately for me, that particular effect is mutual. That's what I'm offering here, Ethan. Love. A love strong enough and true enough to build a life around. One that will last a lifetime. Possibly more. Take it or leave it.'

She slid from his desk and headed for the door, a vision of spirit, seduction and steely determination. 'It's a good deal, Ethan. One that should appeal to the businessman in you as well as the pirate. You should take it.'

CHAPTER TWELVE

PREPARATIONS for the feast of the hungry ghosts began mid-afternoon. Mia had decided to give the ballroom a whirl, to open it up to the newly built decking and the newly planted gardens that ran all the way down to the beach and back. Cloth-covered tables stood end-to-end, ready for the food to come. Whole baked pigs, pineapples, steam buns and roast chicken. She'd brought in caterers, for she had no chef or kitchen staff yet, but she was looking, always looking for them, and maybe amongst the catering staff tonight she would find them. *Take what you want,* Ethan had told her, right before she'd handed him her heart.

The entertainers were setting up on a stage the Kwong contingent had erected that morning. Musicians and dancers, opera singers and acrobats would entertain there this evening. Something for everyone—even the most discerning hungry ghost. Candles lined the walkways and giant joss sticks stood ready for lighting at regular intervals. She'd set aside an area for the fire—an area that tomorrow would become a goldfish pond—but tonight it would be the place to burn offerings to the hungry ghost of choice. Most of the offerings already accumulated were for Yuen Chin, but not all. There were ancestors to honour, passing ghosts to appease. Good luck to court and enjoyment to be taken from giving.

Her father was here somewhere, looking more like the laughing man in the photo that hung on her wall than she'd ever seen him. He'd said he could stay for a week and she knew him too well to think that he'd neglect Fletcher Corp for very long, but he'd be back. He'd be back.

More people started arriving over the course of the afternoon, bringing food and offerings, bringing colour and warmth. Workers' wives she'd met in the sorting room, aunts, uncles and children—children everywhere.

The breeze stirred as dusk crept in. Mia turned on the side chandeliers in the ballroom, delighting in the gasps and the scatter of light through crystal.

'When are you going to turn on the big one?' asked her father from beside her.

'When it's dark,' she said. 'Lady Jordie's looking for you. Something to do with you owing her a lotus cake, a bottle of sherry, and a day's work in her garden. You and Nathaniel Hamilton.'

'Memory like an elephant,' he muttered.

'By the way—I found the elephants, you know. Great-grandfather's elephants. They ended up in Thailand in an elephant retirement village. The hotel's going to be helping with costs.'

'Do your *shareholders* know this?'

'You do now.' Mia grinned. 'How many shares did you pick up, Daddy?'

Her father sighed. 'Fifteen per cent. And I was *going* to give them back to you for your birthday. As it is, I think I'll keep them. This place won't run on love, Mia.

You're going to need guidance.' He shook his head. 'Elephants!'

'Great-grandfather started it. I'm simply continuing a grand and illustrious tradition.' She looked around the ballroom, thrilled by what she saw. The people and the music, the laughter and the dancing. She and Ethan had danced here in the darkness once. Made love in the shadows. She wanted to dance with him again. 'Any idea who owns the other thirty per cent?'

'A shelf company called EN Corporation,' her father said dryly. 'They picked up on your offer five minutes after it hit your broker's desk. Go figure.'

'Guess I'll have to tell Ethan about the elephants, too,' she said. 'Bastard.'

'Does he know you're in love with him?' asked her father with a wry smile.

'I mentioned it today. Using words he could understand.'

'Oh,' said her father, and, after a very long pause, 'How did that go?'

'Hard to say. I was too scared to stick around and find out.' Bravado only went so far. She'd left his office, come straight home and poured herself a medicinal Scotch to help with the trembling.

'So…is he likely to turn up tonight?'

'You're not going to shoot him, are you?'

'Not yet.'

'Oh, good. Because that would be bad. That could conceivably cause a family rift.'

'I'll keep that in mind,' he said dryly.

'As for him turning up tonight…' Mia scanned the faces in the room, but Ethan's wasn't amongst them. 'I'm hoping he will, but the chances of it happening aren't all that great. He had a wife once... She almost destroyed him.'

'I know the feeling.'

Mia glanced at him. Tucked her arm in the crook of his elbow. 'Then you'll know what I'm fighting against. He has a heart just like yours. Beautiful and true and extremely well guarded.'

'He may not come, Mia.'

'I know.' Hearing her father say it took some of the brightness out of the evening. She sighed and looked around. At the gleaming parquetry floor and the intricately plastered ceiling. The pale green hue of the freshly painted walls and the dazzling architectural effect of a long row of arched windows. 'Ayah should have told me this was your childhood home. Or Rajah. Or you. *You* should have told me.'

'Would it have made a difference?'

'Of course it would! I'd have got you here earlier! How was I supposed to know all that stuff in the basement was yours?' She sighed melodramatically, determined to erase the concern that had appeared in her father's eyes when they'd talked of Ethan. 'I think I gave away your push-bike. A black one with the jolly old England sticker on it?'

'You *did* give away my push-bike!'

'Yes, well. It now belongs to the building foreman's grandfather. But I *did* keep your fishing rods. You'll find them in the basement. Oh, look! The puppeteers have arrived. I'd better show them where to set up. The kids are going to love them.'

'Be sure to tell the children to leave the front row seats free,' he said, with a tilt to his lips that promised a smile.

Mia shot him a questioning glance.

'They're for the ghosts.'

More workers and their families arrived as the evening wore on. Rajah saw to the lighting of the joss sticks, the Kwong family saw to the altar and the bonfire. Large bundles of hell money—in mind-boggling denominations—went into the fire first, followed by the various paper gifts people had made for Yuen Chin. Clothes and cars, necklaces and rings. The paper tea set Mia had made for her went in, along with two packets of Penang's finest tea, one of them with a tiny skull and crossbones drawn discreetly on the underside of the packet. Paper goblets went in, along with two bottles of wine, one of them marked with another tiny warning. Mr Kwong Senior had laughed uproariously at that, drawing gazes to them, but none of them was Ethan's.

Mia threw in the paper dagger she'd made, and stood back and watched it burn with no little satisfaction. She did like a woman to have choices. She saved the bouquet of orchids—real ones, for Yuen Chin's sister—for last, tossing them to the fire with a heartfelt wish that somehow, *somehow,* they would reach her.

She found a quiet place after that—a shadowy seat in the garden where she could watch the night unfold. She was proud of what she and Ethan and their team of talented tradesmen had accomplished. Proud of the way the old hotel glowed like a rare and precious jewel. The Cornwallis Hotel, in the heart of Penang, had a heart of its own, and it pulsed to the beat of myriad cultures. She only wished Ethan were here to see it.

Mia searched the faces around her again and again.

She never gave up on the people she loved.

And the night wore on and on.

Ethan strode in from the shadows of the beach, purposefully skirting the various entertainments and tables loaded with food until he came to his destination. The bonfire burned brightly, fuelled by the offerings others had fed it. His offering was tucked under his arm, hastily wrapped, but chosen with care. A fragile white blanket, a real one—only it wasn't a gift for Yuen Chin.

It was for Arianne.

So you can shelter from the cold, Ari. I hope it finds you. He held the blanket to the flames and let go, breathing deep and shoving his hands in his pockets as he watched it burn. Forgiveness didn't come easy to him, would never come easy, but he could manage compassion for Arianne and the love she'd never found. He could manage that.

He turned away as the last of the smoke from the blanket vanished into the air. The old hotel gleamed invitingly, but he wasn't ready to be drawn into it. Not yet. He needed time to settle before he embraced the crowd. Time to gather the courage to do what he'd come here to do.

He stepped back into the shadows, searching for solitude—but he didn't find it. Mia had found it first, her refuge a low garden bench half hidden by the night.

She looked as if she'd stepped out of one of his dreams.

Her hair whipped across her face, blown there by a wayward breeze, and her eyes—those haunting, haunted eyes—regarded him solemnly. She didn't smile. And his stomach clenched.

He'd done his damndest to drive her away. Protecting his heart, never daring to let her in, all the time knowing she was already there, that she'd always been there and that he'd waited a lifetime for her to arrive. He started towards her, unsure of his welcome, and she stood to greet him, her eyes never leaving his face. Waiting, just waiting.

Had he succeeded in driving her away? He didn't know.

She wore a simple black sheath, the gold oval locket, and her heart—that fierce, courageous heart—in her eyes. He'd never seen anything more beautiful.

'I like your dress,' he said.

'Thank you.' Her gaze skidded briefly down his body before returning to his face. Her lips curved ever so slightly. 'I like your tie.'

He wasn't wearing one. 'Did you make your offerings to Yuen Chin?'

'I did. I'm pretty sure she liked the poisoned wine. Mr Kwong Senior certainly did. It burned in an instant.' She looked over at the fire. 'Somehow I don't think your offering was for our long-dead courtesan.'

'No.'

'No.' She smiled at him, but her eyes held the memory of the things he'd told her about Arianne. And the things he hadn't.

'Would you like to know what it was?'

'I think,' she said hesitantly, 'that whatever went into that fire was very private, very personal.'

'You could always ask me a personal question.'

But she shook her head. 'Not this time, Ethan.'

'So…you don't want to know what it was.' He made it a statement.

'I didn't say that. But sometimes I ask too much of the people I love. And there comes a time to stop.'

'I could tell you,' he said.

'Well, you could.' He thought he saw a smile in her eyes, then it was gone. 'But it's not necessary.'

It was necessary. He needed to say the words to someone who'd understand. He needed to say them to Mia. 'It was a blanket. A blanket for Ari.'

Mia's eyes filled with tears. She didn't talk. She just nodded.

'I've forgiven her, Mia. Maybe… Mostly…' He ran a hand through his hair and opted for absolute honesty. 'Working on it.'

'You do good work,' she said shakily.

'Yeah, well. It's been a long time coming.' Now that he'd told her he desperately wanted to talk about something else. He looked around, looked up at the hotel. Saw magic there, and wonder. 'We did a good job.'

'So we did,' she said, her lips curving as she spared a glance for it.

'Mia—' He had no idea how to say what he'd come here to say. 'Will you dance with me?'

'Here?' She looked uncertain.

'Or in there. Wherever you like. I'm voting for the ballroom,' he murmured. 'There's slightly less chance of ending up naked. Naked could be a problem, what with all these people around.'

'Are you *sure* you want to dance?'

'I'm sure I want to hold you.' He held out his hand, with his heart in his throat, and finally, finally, she took it. He'd held hands with her in passion, held hands with her in greed, but this was holding hands of a different kind, and he never wanted it to end.

'You haven't turned the chandelier on,' he said when they stepped into the ballroom.

'I was going to. When it got dark. And then I went outside and forgot all about it.' She looked at the chandelier, looked at him. 'But now that you mention it…I have a surprise for you.'

'Am I going to *like* this surprise?'

'You're going to love it.' Her steps quickened as they headed for the switchboard the electrician had installed the previous day. He hadn't seen it. Hadn't seen the chandelier in action yet at all. Mia, on the other hand, had. 'Sanjay and the electrician got together and brainstormed some options.'

'How *many* options?' he said, studying the switches.

'Dozens,' she said with a grin. 'C'mon, Ethan. What good is a helicopter-sized chandelier if you can't play with it?'

She had a point.

'So…' he said, studying the switch options from left to right. 'What's your preference? A slow and easy build-up to full-strength light? Half-strength light? Quarter-strength? From the centre out? From the outside in? Flashing?' He slid her an incredulous glance. 'You have a *flashing* ten-thousand-piece crystal chandelier?'

Mia smiled archly. 'You want one. I can tell.'

But she didn't set the chandelier to flashing. She set it to a slow and easy build-up to half-strength light and threw the switch. The chandelier came alive, glittering softly, turning the night into an enchantment.

'Dance with me, Mia,' he said gruffly. 'Come dance with me in the light.'

He led her onto the floor and gathered her to him, too desperate for the feel of her against him for subtlety.

'You…ah…seem to be making something of a statement,' she said. as her arms came up to twine around his neck.

'I have another one.' He cleared his throat, searched her eyes. 'I've thought about your offer, Mia. I've thought about nothing else. I can't lose you. I won't. Not this time. So here I am. No ghosts, no guidelines, no holding back. Whatever you want from me, whatever you need. It's yours.'

He saw the tears start to well in her eyes, closed his own eyes so he wouldn't see them fall. 'Don't cry, Mia, please. I've left it too late, haven't I? I've lost you. Again.'

'No,' she whispered raggedly as her hands came round to frame his face, a gentle thumb brushing the corner of his lips. 'No. I'm right here.'

He opened his eyes and Mia stared back at him, a little solemn, a little smiling. Not crying.

'You're not dancing, Ethan.'

'I'm thinking about it,' he said gruffly, his arms tightening around her, bringing her closer to his heart. 'I love you,' he muttered, figuring that if he said it enough he'd get used to the words. 'I'll always love you.'

She pulled back a fraction to search his face with those haunting, unforgettable eyes. 'May I ask you a personal question, Ethan?'

He smiled a little at that. 'You may.'

'I love the words, Ethan. I needed the words. But are you sure? It's not just the memories talking?'

'No,' he muttered, brushing his lips against hers. Her eyes turned dreamy, so he did it again.

'Here and now, Mia. For richer for poorer…in sickness and in health…from this day forward… It's just us.'

* * * * *

CLASSIC

Quintessential, modern love stories
that are romance at its finest.

EXTRA

HPECNM0312

REQUEST YOUR FREE BOOKS!

◆Harlequin *Presents*

2 FREE NOVELS PLUS
2 FREE GIFTS!

PASSION GUARANTEED SEDUCTION

YES! Please send me 2 FREE Harlequin Presents® novels and my 2 FREE gifts (gifts are worth about $10). After receiving them, if I don't wish to receive any more books, I can return the shipping statement marked "cancel." If I don't cancel, I will receive 6 brand-new novels every month and be billed just $4.30 per book in the U.S. or $4.99 per book in Canada. That's a saving of at least 14% off the cover price! It's quite a bargain! Shipping and handling is just 50¢ per book in the U.S. and 75¢ per book in Canada.* I understand that accepting the 2 free books and gifts places me under no obligation to buy anything. I can always return a shipment and cancel at any time. Even if I never buy another book, the two free books and gifts are mine to keep forever.

106/306 HDN FERQ

Name	(PLEASE PRINT)	

Address		Apt. #

City	State/Prov.	Zip/Postal Code

Signature (if under 18, a parent or guardian must sign)

Mail to the **Reader Service:**
IN U.S.A.: P.O. Box 1867, Buffalo, NY 14240-1867
IN CANADA: P.O. Box 609, Fort Erie, Ontario L2A 5X3

Not valid for current subscribers to Harlequin Presents books.

**Are you a current subscriber to Harlequin Presents books
and want to receive the larger-print edition?
Call 1-800-873-8635 or visit www.ReaderService.com.**

* Terms and prices subject to change without notice. Prices do not include applicable taxes. Sales tax applicable in N.Y. Canadian residents will be charged applicable taxes. Offer not valid in Quebec. This offer is limited to one order per household. All orders subject to credit approval. Credit or debit balances in a customer's account(s) may be offset by any other outstanding balance owed by or to the customer. Please allow 4 to 6 weeks for delivery. Offer available while quantities last.

Your Privacy—The Reader Service is committed to protecting your privacy. Our Privacy Policy is available online at www.ReaderService.com or upon request from the Reader Service.

We make a portion of our mailing list available to reputable third parties that offer products we believe may interest you. If you prefer that we not exchange your name with third parties, or if you wish to clarify or modify your communication preferences, please visit us at www.ReaderService.com/consumerschoice or write to us at Reader Service Preference Service, P.O. Box 9062, Buffalo, NY 14269. Include your complete name and address.

HP11B

Taft Bowman knew he'd ruined any chance he'd had for happiness with Laura Pendleton when he drove her away years ago…and into the arms of another man, thousands of miles away. Now she was back, a widow with two small children…and despite himself, he was starting to believe in second chances.

Harlequin Special® Edition® presents a new installment in USA TODAY *bestselling author* RaeAnne Thayne's *miniseries,* THE COWBOYS OF COLD CREEK.

Enjoy a sneak peek of A COLD CREEK REUNION

Available April 2012 from Harlequin® Special Edition®

A younger woman stood there, and from this distance he had only a strange impression, as though she was somehow standing on an island of calm amid the chaos of the scene, the flashing lights of the emergency vehicles, shouts between his crew members, the excited buzz of the crowd.

And then the woman turned and he just about tripped over a snaking fire hose somebody shouldn't have left there.

Laura.

He froze, and for the first time in fifteen years as a firefighter, he forgot about the incident, his mission, just what the hell he was doing here.

Laura.

Ten years. He hadn't seen her in all that time, since the week before their wedding when she had given him back his ring and left town. Not just town. She had left the whole damn country, as if she couldn't run far enough to get away from him.

Some part of him desperately wanted to think he had made some kind of mistake. It couldn't be her. That was just some other slender woman with a long sweep of honey-blond hair and big, blue, unforgettable eyes. But no. It was definitely Laura. Sweet and lovely.

Not his.

He was going to have to go over there and talk to her. He didn't want to. He wanted to stand there and pretend he hadn't seen her. But he was the fire chief. He couldn't hide out just because he had a painful history with the daughter of the property owner.

Sometimes he hated his job.

Will Taft and Laura be able to make the years recede...or is the gulf between them too broad to ever cross?

Find out in
A COLD CREEK REUNION
Available April 2012 from Harlequin® Special Edition®
wherever books are sold.

Celebrate the 30th anniversary
of Harlequin® Special Edition® with a bonus story
included in each Special Edition® book in April!

SPECIAL EDITION

Life, Love and Family

Celebrate the 30th anniversary of Harlequin®
Special Edition® with *USA TODAY*
bestselling author

RaeAnne Thayne

as she captivates readers with
another story from

THE COWBOYS OF COLD CREEK

Ten years ago, Fire Chief Taft Bowman's parents were
murdered and his pain and bitterness drove the love of his
life to walk away. Now widowed, Laura Pendleton Del Fierro
is back and looking to start over. The moment Taft sees
Laura and her children he realizes what he's been missing
the past ten years and becomes determined to convince
Laura that he never stopped loving her.

A COLD CREEK REUNION

Available April 2012 wherever books are sold.

A bonus 30th anniversary story will be included
in each Special Edition® book in April!

ROMANTIC
SUSPENSE

Danger is hot on their heels!